200 HARLEY STREET

Welcome to the luxurious premises of
the exclusive Hunter Clinic, world renowned
in plastic and reconstructive surgery,
set right on Harley Street, the centre of
elite clinical excellence, in the heart of
London's glittering West End!

Owned by two very different brothers,
Leo and Ethan Hunter, the Hunter Clinic
undertakes both cosmetic and reconstructive
surgery. Playboy Leo handles the rich and
famous clients, enjoying the red carpet
glamour of London's A-list social scene
while brooding ex-army doc Ethan
focuses his time on his passion—
transforming the lives of injured war heroes
and civilian casualties of war.

Emotion and drama abound against the
backdrop of one of Europe's most glamorous
cities, as Leo and Ethan work through their
tensions and find women who will change their
lives for ever!

200 HARLEY STREET

*Glamour, intensity, desire—the lives and loves
of London's hottest team of surgeons!*

Dear Reader

I've always loved the Medical Romance™ linked books. Long before I started to write for Mills & Boon® I used to seek out every book in a series and read them from start to finish. There have been some great serials recently, set in Australia and the US, and I couldn't wait until it was time to set a story in the UK again and I might get to be involved.

Taking part in a series is great fun. I was asked about the kind of hero and heroine I would like and I requested a big Scottish hero who looked like Sawyer from *Lost* and a heroine with fake boobs! I was lucky—I got both my requests. Fake boobs are a general no-no in romance novels. If they are there at all they tend to belong to the villainess in the piece. So I was delighted to write about a heroine who, even though she might have been pressured initially, wasn't embarrassed about the decision she'd made and was happy with her new shape.

Mills & Boon® are books that move with the times and reflect the modern women around them. I'm proud to be part of an up-to-date publisher!

Please feel free to contact me via my website: www.scarlet-wilson.com

Scarlet

Praise for Scarlet Wilson:

200 HARLEY STREET: GIRL FROM THE RED CARPET

BY
SCARLET WILSON

Published in Great Britain 2014
by Mills & Boon, an imprint of Harlequin (UK) Limited,
Large Print edition 2014
Eton House, 18-24 Paradise Road,
Richmond, Surrey, TW9 1SR

© 2014 Harlequin Books S.A.

Special thanks and acknowledgement are given to Scarlet Wilson for her contribution to the *200 Harley Street* series

ISBN: 978-0-263-23903-4

Harlequin (UK) Limited's policy is to use papers that are natural, renewable and recyclable products and made from wood grown in sustainable forests. The logging and manufacturing processes conform to the legal environmental regulations of the country of origin.

Printed and bound in Great Britain
by CPI Antony Rowe, Chippenham, Wiltshire

Scarlet Wilson wrote her first story aged eight and has never stopped. Her family have fond memories of *Shirley and the Magic Purse*, with its army of mice, all with names beginning with the letter 'M'. An avid reader, Scarlet started with every Enid Blyton book, moved on to the *Chalet School* series and many years later found Mills & Boon®.

She trained and worked as a nurse and health visitor, and currently works in public health. For her, finding Mills & Boon® Medical Romance™ was a match made in heaven. She is delighted to find herself among the authors she has read for many years.

Scarlet lives on the West Coast of Scotland with her fiancé and their two sons.

Recent titles by the same author:

HER FIREFIGHTER UNDER THE MISTLETOE
ABOUT THAT NIGHT**
THE MAVERICK DOCTOR AND MISS PRIM**
AN INESCAPABLE TEMPTATION
HER CHRISTMAS EVE DIAMOND
A BOND BETWEEN STRANGERS*
WEST WING TO MATERNITY WING!
THE BOY WHO MADE THEM LOVE AGAIN
IT STARTED WITH A PREGNANCY

The Most Precious Bundle of All
**Rebels with a Cause*

These books are also available in eBook format from www.millsandboon.co.uk

DEDICATION

This book is dedicated to the newest addition to our family, Lleyton John Hyndman, a beautiful boy for whom I'm wishing a long, healthy and happy life.

Welcome to the family!

200 HARLEY STREET

*Glamour, intensity, desire—the lives and loves of
London's hottest team of surgeons!*

**For the next four months enter the world of London's
elite surgeons as they transform the lives of their patients
and find love amidst a sea of passions and tensions…!**

Renowned plastic surgeon and legendary playboy
Leo Hunter can't resist the challenge of unbuttoning
the intriguing new head nurse, Lizzie Birch!
200 HARLEY STREET: SURGEON IN A TUX
by Carol Marinelli

Glamorous Head of PR Lexi Robbins is determined
to make gruff, grieving and super-sexy Scottish surgeon Iain MacKenzie
her Hunter Clinic star!
200 HARLEY STREET: GIRL FROM THE RED CARPET
by Scarlet Wilson

Top-notch surgeons and estranged spouses
Rafael and Abbie de Luca find being forced to work together again
tough as their passion is as incendiary as ever!
200 HARLEY STREET: THE PROUD ITALIAN
by Alison Roberts

One night with his new colleague, surgeon Grace Turner, sees
former Hollywood plastic surgeon Mitchell Cooper daring to live again…
200 HARLEY STREET: AMERICAN SURGEON IN LONDON
by Lynne Marshall

Injured war hero Prince Marco meets physical therapist
Becca Anderson—the woman he once shared a magical *forbidden*
summer romance with long ago…
200 HARLEY STREET: THE SOLDIER PRINCE
by Kate Hardy

When genius micro-surgeon Edward North meets single mum
Nurse Charlotte King she opens his eyes to a whole new world…
200 HARLEY STREET: THE ENIGMATIC SURGEON
by Annie Claydon

Junior surgeon Kara must work with hot-shot
Irish surgeon Declan Underwood—the man she kissed at the hospital ball!
200 HARLEY STREET: THE SHAMELESS MAVERICK
by Louisa George

Brilliant charity surgeon Olivia Fairchild faces the man who once
broke her heart—damaged ex-soldier Ethan Hunter. Yet she's unprepared
for his haunted eyes and the shock of his sensual touch…!
200 HARLEY STREET: THE TORTURED HERO by Amy Andrews

**Experience glamour, tension, heartbreak and emotion
at 200 HARLEY STREET
in this new eight-book continuity
from Mills & Boon® Medical Romance™**

**These books are also available in eBook format
and in two 200 HARLEY STREET collection bundles
from www.millsandboon.co.uk**

CHAPTER ONE

LEXI TAPPED HER pink fingernails on the desk with impatience. The clinic was in complete darkness. All caused by a little '*phoof*' when she'd tried to switch on the lights in one of the consulting rooms. If only she knew where the main trip switch was.

She squinted at her watch, using the light from her phone. Just after eleven o'clock at night. Where was he? He had to be here somewhere—his car was parked just down the road. She'd already phoned the few members of staff that were currently in Drake's wine bar and he wasn't with them.

She spun on her heel, a new determination causing her stomach to clench.

'Iain McKenzie, you can run but you can't hide.'

He'd been avoiding her all day.

She knew that.

And he knew that.

But two could play at that game. No one escaped Lexi Robbins, Head of PR at the Hunter Clinic. She'd got tired of dodging his lame excuses via his devoted and sergeant-majorish secretary. She'd looked at his theatre lists today and knew exactly when he'd be available.

Except he'd been in a meeting, then taking a conference call, then out buying a sandwich. The final straw had been when his secretary had said he'd left to pick up his dry-cleaning!

So she'd waited. Lexi Robbins could be very patient. She was also very persistent. So far she'd been through the three operating theatres, the recovery room and the anaesthetic room—even though there were no patients in the building— all in her search for Iain.

She'd checked his room four times today. She'd checked the waiting room, the kitchen, the changing rooms and the treatment rooms. She'd been down to the gym and private swimming pool too—the thought of catching Iain McKenzie in a state of undress wasn't exactly unappealing. Now she'd started checking the *other* consultants' rooms in the hope she'd catch him hiding somewhere.

As a kid she'd been the best at hide and seek and she'd no intention of being beaten now.

Iain McKenzie had met his match.

It was infuriating. *He* was infuriating. She was only trying to do her job and help raise the profile of the clinic to try and attract some more overseas clients. So far, she'd managed to persuade several celebrity friends, a few TV film stars, an international politician and the sheikh of Amal to use the services of the Hunter Clinic. Interviewing and filming some of the staff members would help her publicity drive to even bigger audiences.

And with his shaggy hair, muscular build and Scottish accent Iain McKenzie was to die for. Women would love him and flock to this clinic from miles around if only she could get him on screen and online.

She'd worked hard for this job and had no intention of failing. Leo Hunter had just let her know that they were linking with a charity, so raising the profile and income of the Hunter Clinic would be even more crucial than before. She was determined not to let him down, not when he'd given her an opportunity that others hadn't.

Being the daughter of a family constantly in the media meant she had her own cross to bear. If she had a pound for every time someone had said the words 'You're Penelope Crosby's daughter?', usually with an expression of disbelief in their eyes, she would never need to work again. Being the daughter of a former famous model with one of the world's top-selling range of beauty products was tough—having a father who interviewed all the top celebrities in the world, along with his billionaire status, was even tougher.

No one in her family had respected her decision to go to university and get her degree. No one in the family respected the work she did at the Hunter Clinic. The only time her parents had ever been happy with her choices was when she'd spent a few summers doing charity work because it had given them more good publicity than they would ever need.

That's why she was so determined not to let Leo down.

No matter how hard Iain McKenzie tried to hide from her.

She could see it in her head right now. The publicity shot she wanted to use—Iain McKenzie in that dark grey suit he wore, with a white shirt and red tie, arms folded across his chest in front of the Hunter Clinic sign. He would look fabulous.

Or maybe she should put him in a set of navy scrubs—all his athletic muscles would be clearly on show. Or maybe she could persuade him to wear a kilt.

No. Scratch that. Old prickly guts would never agree to wear a kilt for her.

She pushed open the door to Mitchell Cooper's room. Even though the lights were out there was plenty of light from the outside streetlights in Harley Street. She could see around the room easily. Empty. Just like all the others.

There was only one place left. Leo Hunter's office. The boss.

She felt a flutter of excitement. Leo's office was the most gorgeous in the building. Spectacular views over Harley Street, hand-picked opulent furniture and gorgeous soft furnishings.

She turned the handle carefully. It almost felt wrong, creeping into the boss's office while he wasn't around. But she was determined to check every inch of this clinic.

But something was wrong. There were no gentle lights from the street bathing the office in a partly orange glow.

The curtains were pulled tightly, leaving the office in complete darkness. She fumbled with her phone, trying to pull it from her pocket and use the torch to see her way around.

A flicker of nerves danced across her skin. What was that faint noise? She held her breath, leaning forward a little and straining to hear. But after more than sixteen hours in stiletto heels her balance had deserted her. She tripped on the large Turkish rug Leo kept in the middle of his floor. She fell forward and let out a gasp, reaching out towards the blackness in front of her and hitting the edge of the chesterfield lounge—and a whole lot more.

There was movement. Sudden, powerful movement and none of it was hers. Lexi felt the breath leave her body as she found herself spun around and pushed flat on her back onto the chesterfield lounge.

Her heart pounded in her chest, the thudding reverberating in her ears. She tried to reach out and fight her attacker as an adrenaline surge hit her body. Fight or flight had never seemed more apt. But the arms holding her down were fierce. Fierce and strong, very strong.

Her breath seemed caught in her throat, her tongue stuck to the roof of her mouth. Her attacker's weight was pressing down on her chest, affecting her ability to take a deep breath.

She still couldn't see. It was just darkness, pure and utter darkness. Like your worst nightmare and most hated horror movie all rolled into one.

She heard a grunt. And it gave her the faintest glimmer of hope.

It was a grunt she thought she recognised.

Usually when she was trying to persuade him to acknowledge her existence.

She fought to push the word from her throat. 'Iain?' she croaked.

Iain had finally managed to grab a few minutes' precious sleep. There was no point in going home. No matter how exhausted he was—or how many hours he'd spent in theatre, making the world look 'more beautiful'—sleep evaded him the second he stepped through his doorway.

Too much quiet. Too much time to let his brain spin around and around, going over all aspects of his past. Every decision made, every conversation, every cross word, every pleaded case. If only he'd taken the road less travelled.

It didn't matter that he'd moved from Edinburgh to London. His house had too many memories and too many familiar knick-knacks that he couldn't face putting away. That would be like a betrayal.

So he'd spent half the day playing cat and mouse with Lexi Robbins. The woman wouldn't give him a moment's peace. Boy, was she tenacious—his gran would have loved her. All over an interview that he'd cancelled at the last minute and publicity that he couldn't really care less about.

And just when the muscles in his body had finally started to relax—just when the last remnants of tension had finally managed to exit his body—this.

Noise. In the Hunter Clinic in the middle of the night.

Noise. In a place where he was supposed to be alone.

The assailant was smaller than he expected. Lighter than he expected too. Probably in search of drugs or the elusive cosmetic fillers that Harley Street was so famous for.

Then it hit him. That smell.

The smell that had been haunting him around the clinic for the last few days.

Strike that. Actually, for the last few months. Ever since Lexi Robbins had started working there.

Sensual woody amber distinctive notes with gentle floral notes of jasmine. Along with the feel of some very distinctive soft curves that only a plastic surgeon could recognise merely by touch.

He could feel the assailant's soft breath beneath him, along with the strangled voice. 'Iain?'

'Lexi?' He sprang backwards, moving swiftly to the door and trying to flick on the light. Nothing. Still darkness.

'I think I blew the lights,' came the whisper from the couch. She was still breathless. He'd obviously winded her.

After a few seconds she fumbled for her phone and pressed the button to light up the room. She held it towards him. 'Do you know where the master switch is?'

Rage was circulating in his belly. What on earth was she doing? He snatched the phone from her hand and strode down the corridor towards the electricity box, opening it quickly and flicking the master switch, allowing instant illumination in parts of the clinic.

Bright. White. Everywhere.

Sometimes he could groan out loud about the décor in the clinic. Leo Hunter had wanted brilliant white and clean lines everywhere—thank goodness he'd been allowed to decorate his office to his own taste.

But now that he could actually see what he was doing he was furious.

'What were you thinking of, Lexi?' He stormed back into the room.

But Lexi hadn't moved. Even though the room was now flooded with light she was still lying on the couch, her hands pressed to her chest, her face as white as a sheet. One shoe was twisted on the floor , the other dangling from the end of her foot. Her usually pristine suit was a little askew and it looked as if the top button had popped from her shirt.

Yikes! He'd thought he was tackling a burglar. Maybe he'd been a little more forceful than he thought.

'Lexi? Are you okay?' He stood over her, giving her a few seconds to collect herself.

After what seemed like an age she finally blinked. Colour flooded into her face and she pushed herself up. 'Wow. Talk about sweeping the legs from under a girl.'

Iain felt colour come to his own cheeks. He was trying hard not to stare at Lexi's cleavage. He was a plastic surgeon. He spent his days with his hands on women's breasts. But he'd never clocked Lexi Robbins as a boob job kind of girl. She'd surprised him.

In all the time she'd been around him in the last few months, wearing her designer suits, he'd never noticed her additions. But then again, he'd never seen her undressed.

He pushed the thoughts that sprang to mind aside instantly. He sat down on one of the leather armchairs and put his head in his hands. 'What on earth are you doing here at this time of night, Lexi?' He was tired. And he was definitely feeling crabbit.

She straightened on the couch, looking down at her shirt and frowning at the missing button. 'I could ask you the same thing.'

She was obviously feeling a bit better. Lexi Robbins could give as good as she got. He raised his eyebrows at her and gave her a cheeky smile. 'Avoiding you?'

She shot him a glare.

He held up his hands. 'Seriously, Lexi. I thought you were a burglar. You're lucky I didn't do you some permanent damage.'

'Who says you didn't?'

She was adjusting herself on the couch and he felt instantly uncomfortable. What did she mean? He hadn't done anything more than push her onto the couch and hold her down. There was no way he could have damaged her implants.

Her blonde tousled hair fell over her face as she shuffled on the edge of the couch. Iain was torn between panic and embarrassment. It didn't help that his curiosity was naturally piqued.

He'd heard of Lexi before she'd started work here. Even for a man who had as little interest in celebrities as humanly possible—other than to contemplate what procedures they'd had done—it was impossible to miss Lexi Robbins.

If there was an event she was at it. Albeit usually trying to fade into the background behind her mother and father, but dazzling all the same. He'd instantly dismissed her as a wannabe and had been more than a little surprised when Leo had hired her as their head of PR.

But Leo Hunter only hired the best. And Iain could vouch for that as Leo had pursued him relentlessly to get him here.

She lifted her head and gave her hair a shake, catching him with her blue eyes and winking. 'Gotcha!'

He couldn't stop the instant smile that appeared on his lips. Even this late at night, after pursuing him all day, she could still joke with him.

She slid off the chesterfield and moved over towards him, folding her arms across her depleted shirt. 'So, Iain McKenzie, your mission to avoid me has failed. Resistance is futile.'

He raised his eyebrows. Surprised by her knowledge of his favourite TV show. Lexi Robbins did her homework.

'You're going to have to agree to the interview *and* to me shadowing you for a few days. I mean, after all, some people could be very upset about being mishandled.'

He sighed. 'Ms Robbins, are you trying to blackmail me?'

She gave a perfunctory nod. 'You bet I am.'

He shook his head. 'Lexi, find someone else. Some happy, shiny person who likes doing this kind of thing. I just want to do my job.'

'And so do I. Believe it or not, Ethan Hunter is even more difficult than you. Would you call him happy and shiny? Because he's my other potential interviewee.' She raised her eyebrows at him.

His head was spinning. She'd moved closer and he was getting a waft of that perfume again. Predator perfume. At least that was what his brain was telling him.

It was making him uneasy, on edge. Or maybe it was just reminding him of how up close and personal they'd just been.

When was the last time he'd been up close and personal with a woman?

He didn't even want to think about that. He'd known from the second he'd laid eyes on her that Lexi Robbins meant trouble for him. His body reacted in ways it shouldn't when she was around. The sound of her voice, the smell of her distinctive perfume, even the sound of her stiletto heels clicking along the corridor were enough to send his imagination into overdrive and remind him of why he'd been avoiding her at all costs.

He rubbed his sleep-heavy eyes. Maybe his nightmares had taken a new turn and an alien was about to burst from her stomach and eat him alive. Nope. She was still there. Still staring at him with her big blue eyes and pink lips.

She held out her hand towards him.

'What?'

'Let's go, Iain.'

For a second he was confused. 'Go where?'

She shot him a dazzling smile. 'Home. I'm going to take you home.'

CHAPTER TWO

SHE WAS TRYING not to show her nerves. Trying to pretend that this was an everyday occurrence.

But Iain McKenzie wasn't helping. His brow was wrinkled, deep furrowed wrinkles that marred his handsome complexion.

She leaned forward and grabbed hold of one his hands, bending down in front of him. 'Iain, I'm worried about you. You spent hours in surgery today, then you spent another few hours avoiding me, and now I catch you here...' she held up her other hand '...fast asleep in another office.' She looked up into his face, seeing tiny lines of exhaustion around his eyes that instantly tugged at her heart. 'It's not good, Iain. You are one of our greatest assets. I wouldn't be doing my job if I didn't take you home.'

The confused and uptight expression on his

face relaxed a little. Oh, no. What had he thought she'd meant?

She patted his hand. It was meant to be reassuring, motherly. But it wasn't working for her, and she doubted it was working for him. It was only making her sluggish veins pick up tempo and send the blood flowing more quickly back to her heart.

The long day had obviously caused her brain to become fuddled. The sooner she got Iain McKenzie home safely the better.

He stood up next to her and she was instantly swamped by his large athletic frame. 'Don't be silly, Lexi. You're not going to drive me home. My car is down the street. I'll go and get it.'

That accent. That Scottish burr sent shivers down her spine. She could happily listen to it all day. And she could bet that potential clients could too. She had to persuade him to take part in the publicity campaign. Iain was pure gold.

It was time for a firm approach. 'Iain, I meant what I said. From what I can gather, you've put in a sixteen-hour day so far. You were sleeping soundly before I disturbed you.' Then she wrinkled her nose. 'And, truth be told, I'd already staked out your car. It looks as if it's got a flat. There's no way you're changing that at this time of night.' She gave a little laugh. 'Not in the dark anyway, with those surgeon's hands. How much are they worth?'

She saw his shoulders sag a little and it gave her a spurt of hope. Maybe tomorrow he could forgive her little white lie? In the meantime, she had to use her best tactics to persuade him to take part in the publicity.

He gave his forehead another rub and arched his back. 'Okay, Lexi. Thanks for the offer. I guess spending the night in the clinic isn't ideal.' He bent over and picked up his jacket, which was lying across a chair, then held the door open for her.

She gave a little nod, straightened her blouse and jacket and slipped her feet back into her shoes. It only took a few minutes to reach her car, which she'd moved near the clinic entrance.

He nodded in approval. 'Sports car? Nice, Lexi. Did you pick this yourself?'

She gave an embarrassed shake of her head as

she pressed the button to open the doors. 'Not exactly. It was a birthday present.'

He let out a sigh as he sat down in the passenger seat, folding his long legs into the small footwell. 'That's some birthday present. From a man?'

The question hung in the air between them. Was he curious about her love life, or was he just making small talk? The air in the car seemed to instantly close around them as she slammed her door. Iain McKenzie was a big man in the small space. The sleeve of his jacket was brushing against hers.

Her brain was ready to drift back to the office. To the feel of the hard planes of his chest against her firm breasts.

She pushed the gearstick into reverse and looked at him sideways. 'The car was from my father. I'd like to think he spent hours thinking about it, but the reality is his PA probably picked the make, model and colour and all he had to do was sign the cheque.'

She pulled out into the street. It was practically empty at this time in the morning and her natural instinct was to floor it. Talking about her parents brought out the worst in her.

Iain surprised her. He let out a deep, hearty laugh. She glanced over, raising her eyebrows in surprise.

'So you're a cynic, then, Lexi Robbins. I never had you down for that. I thought you lived a re-markably charmed life.'

Her instant reaction was to bristle and put him promptly in his place. But this was her chance to work on him—not alienate him. Plus with that face she was still curious as to why a man as hard working and good looking as Iain didn't have someone to rush home to. Why on earth would anyone like him want to sleep at the clinic? It just didn't make sense.

'I know you've been avoiding me. I'm not an idiot, you know.'

'I'm sorry. I just don't have the time. And to be honest, I can't really see the point. Get some-one else to do it. Someone who likes a bit of the limelight on them.'

'Like who, Ethan?'

She let the question hang in the air. If Iain was

prickly then Ethan Hunter was a floating under-water mine.

A former soldier, who was still recuperating from an injury he really refused to acknowledge. His heart was in the right place and he was committed to all the charity work the clinic was involved in—most of it he'd referred himself. But putting Ethan on screen for the clinic's publicity would be a complete no-no. She'd already tried to interview him twice with no success. Ethan just wasn't a people person.

Whatever had happened in his past meant he just wasn't ready for this kind of thing, and Lexi knew enough about people to know when to leave it alone. Hence her relentless pursuit of Iain. He was her current golden goose—whether he liked it or not.

Iain eventually let out a long sigh. 'Okay. Agreed, Ethan probably isn't the best person right now. He asked me to be involved in his charity work and obviously I agreed—who wouldn't? I can make a real difference to some of those patients' lives. I'm happy to help. I'm happy to give up my time and do the surgery free. It's just the rest of the stuff I don't like so much.'

Lexi lifted her hands off the steering-wheel of the car and made quote marks with her fingers in the air. 'You mean the "rest of the stuff" like me?'

Iain ran his fingers through his dark hair. It was obvious he was tired and she was putting him on the spot. But maybe, just maybe, in a moment of weakness he would relent and agree to what she wanted.

She indicated and turned the car into the nearest street. It would only be a few more minutes before they reached Iain's townhouse. It was time to turn the screw. 'I don't think you understand how hard I'm working at all this, Iain. You might do the surgery for free, but what about everything else? We need to pay for theatre time, equipment use, other staff salaries and all the aftercare. We need the publicity to raise funds for all other aspects of the charity work. These interviews are really important.

'Leo has just agreed to take on another charity for one of his friends. Did he talk to you about

Fair Go—Olivia Fairchild's charity? She's doing some stellar work in Africa. There are children out there who really need our help. Kids who've been victims of the violence—victims of war. The kind of kids who fall through the cracks. Their conditions aren't life-threatening or emergencies—but think of the difference we could make to their lives by doing what in this country would be seen as basic surgery. If we can do some interviews with staff members, focus on their special skills and surgeries, get the information out there for the world and media to see, it could really raise the profile of the Hunter Clinic. The more international customers we have, the more disposable income the clinic can use to help aid these charities.

'The Hunter Clinic has finally managed to regain its reputation and polish. Things are looking even better now people know that Leo and Ethan are working together. It does wonders for the whole ethos of the place. Just think, Iain, if a clinic that's known as the best of the best is going all out for some of these charities, don't you think that will make people stop and think?

It'll make people look more closely at these charities and wonder what they could do to help too. That's exactly the kind of publicity that they need, Iain. This isn't just about your surgical skills and time, it's about the bigger picture. It's about what everyone else can do to help.'

She couldn't stop the enthusiasm and passion that was coming through in her voice. She was excited just thinking about this and the huge realm of possibilities. She could tell she was getting to him. He wasn't so quick to answer back, as if he were mulling over what she'd just said. Exactly the way she'd hoped he would.

Her brain was whirring again and her tongue itching to fill the silence in the car. But this was exactly the time to be quiet. To leave him with no excuse but to mull it over.

She changed gear and her hand brushed against his thigh. Wow. Now there were a hundred reasons for a girl not to concentrate on the road.

For a second she felt a little panicked. She could smell him. His scent was invading her senses and she was starting to feel swamped by his presence in her car. She could remember his firm hands on her shoulders, holding her down on the couch. It had been terrifying. All rational thought had flown out of the window.

Of course it had to have been Iain. He was the person she'd been hunting for in the clinic—who else could it possibly have been?

And once the terror had left her, all she'd been left with had been the whoosh.

That feeling of being close to a man again. How long had it been since she'd let a man touch her? And how much had her senses fired in Iain's powerful arms?

She tried to shake the intimate thoughts from her head. She was a professional. She had a job to do. And Iain McKenzie was part of that job.

Her PR head started to buzz. Should she have concerns about Iain McKenzie? Why on earth was one of their top surgeons sleeping at the clinic? She'd read the information in his personnel file. She knew he was originally from Edinburgh and had a broad general experience before specialising in plastics. He'd printed several professional papers, spoke at conferences and conducted scientific clinical studies into different techniques for various types of plastic surgery. Technically, he was brilliant.

So why did she feel as if something was wrong? More importantly, why did it make her stomach twist?

That was the thing about Iain's personnel file. There was hardly a 'personal' thing in it. All professional. It just didn't sit right with her.

She pulled up outside his townhouse.

'How did you know where I stay, Lexi? I never told you.'

The frown was etched on his brow again. If he wasn't careful it would become a permanent fixture.

She smiled. 'I'm the Head of PR, Iain. I know everything about everybody.' She looked up at the dark townhouse. It wasn't exactly welcoming.

Bleak and sombre. A bit like Iain.

She'd expected him to more or less jump from the car the second they arrived but he didn't. He sat for a few moments then turned to face her. With so little space between them in the car she was almost afraid to turn round.

'I appreciate what you're trying to do for the charities. Really, I do, Lexi. And if Leo hired you then he must think you're good at your job.'

'And you don't?' Was that the implication? Because that train of thought alarmed her.

He shook his head and lifted his hand. 'Don't be so defensive. What exactly is it you want from me?'

She took a deep breath. Finally. She was going to get somewhere with him.

'I want to shadow you for a few days. See your consultations with patients. Watch you perform surgery. Once I've had a chance to get to see the real you, I'll interview you on camera. It will work better that way, I'll know you—you'll know me. The interview will go more smoothly.'

He frowned. 'That's a bit more in-depth than I expected. I can't have you disturbing things with my patients. If they don't want you around you have to leave.' His words were absolutely definite.

She nodded quickly. 'Agreed.'

'And I'll need my patients' consent for you to watch any surgeries.'

'Will that be difficult?'

He let out a slow stream of air through his lips. 'Not tomorrow it won't. I'm performing surgery on Aida Atkins. You know how fame-hungry she is. She'll be falling all over herself at the mere thought of some publicity for herself.' He paused. 'You signed a confidentiality agreement when you started at the clinic?'

She nodded.

'I think you'll find with Aida Atkins you may as well throw it out the window.'

Aida Atkins. The latest model-cum-actress-cum-trophy wife. Lexi had seen more of them than she'd eaten home-cooked meals. Hardly difficult.

'This publicity is really about the clinic, the work you do and the associated charities.'

'Aida won't care. If she gets her five minutes of fame she'll be happy. Her type are all the same.'

'What does that mean?' There was a horrible little gnawing feeling at the pit of her stomach. She could almost predict what he was about to say.

'Vain. Pretentious. Fixed ideas about what a perfect body should look like.'

'If you feel like that, why are you operating on her?'

'Because it's what she wants. Because she's medically and psychologically competent to make a decision about surgery and she's not an anaesthetic risk. As simple as that.'

Lexi could feel a wave of disappointment sweep over her body. Was that what he thought about all his plastic-surgery clients? That they were all superficial and vain? Was that what he thought about her because she'd had a boob job?

He shook his head as if he realised his words sounded unnecessarily harsh. 'Wait until tomorrow. You'll understand then. There's a reason I'm doing Aida's surgery instead of a general plastic surgeon.'

Iain put his hand on the door handle. 'Princess Catherine's. Seven a.m. tomorrow. And bring something to eat. It will be a long day.' It took him a few seconds to release his long legs from the foot well. He straightened up and pulled some house keys from his pocket.

She watched as he looked over at the house. There was no look of relief to finally be home. More a look of resignation. He bent back down. 'Thanks for the lift, Lexi. See you tomorrow.' Then he slammed the door and trudged up his steps.

Lexi took a deep breath. There was so much more hidden behind the handsome façade of Iain McKenzie. The question was, how much did she want to find out?

CHAPTER THREE

THE DARKNESS PERVADED him as soon as he set foot in his house. It was such a shame as it was a beautiful home and, in theory, all his dark memories should have been left behind in Edinburgh.

Coming to London was supposed to be the start of something new for him. He just couldn't seem to shake off the big black thundercloud of guilt that hung permanently above his head.

He flicked on a light and looked out at the road. Lexi hadn't pulled away yet. Should he have invited her in? Had he been impolite? It had been so long since he'd done any of the social niceties with women that he'd probably forgotten what most of them were.

He watched as she indicated and pulled out onto the quiet street. It was after midnight. If he'd invited her in it might have been misconstrued as something else entirely. And whether he admitted it or not, he was trying to avoid the woman who was causing uncomfortable flarings in his libido, not invite her into his home.

He paused at the dark polished sideboard, which held a photograph of himself and his wife, Bonnie. They were sitting on the grass in their garden in Edinburgh, her back leaning against him and his arms wrapped around her enlarged abdomen. Bonnie had the most contented look on her face. The look of a woman who had finally got the thing she'd always dreamed of. They *both* looked like that, but Iain knew the truth behind that photo.

One of his friends had suggested he put that picture away. A friend who'd been close enough to both of them to know what had actually happened.

But Iain couldn't do that. His guilt didn't matter. This was still his favourite picture of them both. They looked so relaxed. They looked so happy. As if they had their whole lives ahead of them.

If only he'd known…

His fingers touched the glass in front of the

photograph. 'Three years, Bonnie,' he whispered. And not a single day had gone by that he hadn't thought of her.

They'd been childhood sweethearts. Destined to be together for ever. Or so they had thought.

When Leo Hunter had pursued him to work at the Hunter Clinic he'd thought the guy was crazy. His world had just collapsed around him and Leo had wanted him to up sticks and move to another part of the country?

But Leo had understood him better than he'd understood himself. He'd known he would never be able to pull himself up if he stayed in the family home, with the same work colleagues with their averted eyes and sad expressions. The move to London had been exactly what he'd needed at the time. Apart from Leo, no one knew about his wife. He'd skirted around the edges of any potentially difficult conversations, avoiding any personal details.

London was easy to lose yourself in. And the clientele coming to and from the Hunter Clinic had more to worry about than the personal background of their surgeon. And it was better that way. It really was.

Iain walked into his vast kitchen and pulled a glass from the cupboard, pressing it against the dispenser on his stainless-steel fridge. A beautiful kitchen that he hardly used. Just like the rest of this house.

He climbed the staircase to his bedroom, peeled off his jacket, trousers, shirt and tie, not bothering to hang them up. He'd have to be up in a few hours to get to Princess Catherine's for surgery and he had a whole rail of identical business suits in the cupboard.

He sank into the bed with white Egyptian cotton sheets. Praying that tonight—even for a few hours—he might get a few hours' precious sleep.

But it wasn't to be.

It seemed that it wasn't only the scent of Lexi Robbins that had pervaded his memory. He sat bolt upright in bed, sweat pouring from his body.

This was why he'd purposefully been avoiding Lexi Robbins.

He'd known it. Right from the first time he'd seen her and he'd felt a skitter of impulses across his shoulders that he couldn't be around her. He couldn't be near her.

He leant forward and wiped the sweat from his brow. Erotic dreams weren't the norm for Iain. But when Lexi's firm breasts had pressed against the planes of his chest it had left an indelible imprint. Not just on his skin.

Those tiny, fleeting thoughts that hadn't even taken up a second in his brain when he'd had her pressed down on the examination couch had just taken front and centre stage in his mind in all their erotic beauty. Dreams like that had more than one obvious effect on the body.

He'd never be able to look Lexi Robbins in the eye today. It was almost as if he could smell her here, now.

He jumped from the bed and walked through to the en suite, flicking the switch on the shower then coming back and gulping the glass of water at the side of his bed. Was he going crazy? He *could* smell Lexi Robbins.

Then he remembered how close they'd been. He snatched his crumpled shirt from the floor and pressed it to his nose. There. Not the smell of his own aftershave. The smell of her.

That heady, exotic smell that left an invisible pied-piper trail wherever she went. That was what had caused the dream. Nothing else.

The shirt had been lying at his bedside and her scent had obviously drifted up and around him while he'd slept. How could this woman find a way into his dreams?

Guilt flooded through him, seeping in through every pore on his body. The hot sweat instantly turned cold, chilling his skin. Bonnie. That's who he should have been dreaming about. No one else.

Steam was starting to billow from the shower. He stalked back through and instantly turned the switch to cold. That was what he needed. Icy, cold, blasting water to wash away any unwanted thoughts or feelings.

He stepped into the freezing water, shuddering as it came into contact with his skin. There was no point going back to sleep now.

Not if Lexi Robbins was going to feature in his dreams again.

CHAPTER FOUR

'MORNING, MORNING.' LEXI nodded at the sea of faces in and around the theatres at Princess Catherine's, or Kate's, where the Hunter Clinic had an arrangement to perform adult surgery. Children's surgery was carried out at the Lighthouse Children's Hospital.

Lexi had thought she'd be in good stead, turning up early. But early seemed to be normal in the theatres here.

She'd followed all the instructions carefully. Even though she wouldn't be near any patients, she'd removed the nail varnish from her fingernails, ensured her face was scrubbed clean of any make-up and left her perfume and jewellery at home. She didn't want to give Iain McKenzie any reason not to let her shadow him today.

And her stomach was churning a little. Nerves. Lots of them. Most of the world saw Lexi Robbins as a together, sorted woman. She didn't reveal the insecure woman that hid away underneath. The person who was horrified to be here with a bare face and pulled-back hair.

It was odd, but she felt strangely safe here. No paparazzi were going to jump out from a corner and snap her, showing the world she wasn't as beautiful as her mother. No one here cared. Everyone here had one purpose in mind—excellent patient care. It was almost a relief to know she could fade into the background.

Kate's was buzzing. There was a rainbow of coloured scrubs around her. She'd been under the illusion that everyone wore the same-coloured scrubs, but Kate's had scrubs in every colour, shape and size. One of the theatre nurses had pointed her to a laundry cupboard and told her to help herself. So she had, and she was currently sporting pale pink scrubs and white clogs.

'Ready?'

The deep voice behind her made her jump. 'Oh, Iain. Great. I was waiting for you.'

The words seemed to come out all wrong and she could feel the colour rushing into her face.

She might have guessed it. Even dressed in navy scrubs there was no disguising his broad frame and muscles. If she was going to have to watch that muscled back all day she might as well just go and lie down in a corner now.

'I've already spoken to Aida. She signed a disclaimer. She's more than happy for you to watch her surgery—you can even film it if you like.'

Lexi cleared her throat. 'Actually, it's you we would be filming, Iain. We don't intend to focus on the patient. Just let people see your expertise at work.'

'Whatever.' He gave a shrug and pushed open the door to the theatre. 'After you…'

She nodded and brushed past his arm as he held the door open for her. *No contact*. That's what she'd been telling herself all night. Seems like she'd broken her first rule already.

She tried to back herself into a corner as the rest of the staff moved in perfect unison around the theatre. Iain and one of his colleagues scrubbing meticulously at the sinks. The nurses opening up theatre packs, the anaesthetist and his assistant bringing Aida into Theatre and talking to her quietly and calmly as they put her under.

Lexi could feel herself holding her breath as the drapes were placed around Aida and her skin cleaned with betadine. Wow. Scars like she'd never seen before.

Iain's brown eyes connected with hers above his mask. He nodded towards her. 'Step a little closer, Lexi.'

Her feet moved forward, even though her body wanted to remain pinned against the wall.

'This is the reason that Aida isn't being operated on by a general plastic surgeon.' His gloved hand pointed at her scarring. 'She has significant scarring caused by her previous surgery. This operation isn't just about replacing her implants, it's about reducing the scarring and trying to give her the best possible outcome.'

Lexi nodded behind her mask. 'Why does she have scars like that?'

Iain spoke slowly. 'All patients react differently to surgery. Some form thick, keloid scars, others hypertrophic scars like these. It's to do with collagen in the skin. The most important aspect for Aida isn't what I do today—although that's obviously important—it's more about her aftercare to minimise scarring.'

'But if she's prone to scarring, is there anything you can do to avoid it?'

'We'll monitor Aida very closely. We can use various things after surgery to reduce inflammation and scarring. A series of steroid injections might be appropriate or silicone gel sheeting used to flatten the scar. Aida knows that she has to follow my instructions to the letter for her aftercare. It was the only reason I agreed to do her surgery in the first place.'

Lexi could feel the hairs rise at the back of her neck. Iain wasn't joking. She could just imagine how stern he'd been with Aida before agreeing to her surgery. The scarring was a complete surprise to her. She was sure she'd seen semi-naked pictures of Aida before, and nothing had been noticeable. How had she managed that?

Of course. The beauty of photographic touch-ups. She knew better than anyone how fickle the beauty industry was. As long as they got the picture they wanted it didn't matter how they got it—or whether it was an accurate portrayal of the person or not.

Her feet moved slowly backwards, edging towards the wall again. She wished she'd known about the surgery beforehand and had given herself a little time to prepare. Watching breast surgery and having breast surgery were two entirely different things. In a way she was glad she'd slept through her own surgery and had never had to think too much about it all. She had to press her hands against the cool wall to stop herself automatically lifting them and holding them against her breasts.

She glanced downwards. There they were. Perfect, in every way.

If only she'd got them because *she*'d wanted them and not because someone else had criticised her. It almost made her feel like a fool.

But she was stronger now. More resilient.

She was happy with her shape and regardless of anyone else's opinion she had more confidence like this.

Iain's concentration was intense in Theatre. Woe betide anyone who interrupted the master at work. But the theatre staff were comfortable with him, obviously used to his techniques and procedures. He hardly needed to utter an instruction.

The surgery flew past. Quickly followed by another, more standard breast enlargement. He turned to face her as he scrubbed for yet another surgery.

'Now would be a good time to grab a quick bite,' he said to Lexi.

As if on cue, her stomach gave a low rumble. 'Haven't you finished yet?'

He shook his head. 'Not by a long shot. I've got some reconstructive surgery to do on a professional football player's knee and then some facial surgery on a lady with head and neck cancer. That one will last around four hours.'

Lexi tried to stop her jaw from hitting the floor when she realised exactly how long Iain would be in Theatre. 'I didn't know you did things like that. If that surgery will take so long, shouldn't it have been done first?'

He gave a little nod of acknowledgement. 'You're right. We normally do the most complicated surgery first but Carol Kennedy has enough on her plate. She wanted to keep things as normal as possible. She wanted to drop her kids at school today and has told them that she's got business in the city for a few days.'

Lexi felt a little tug at her heart as she recognised the name of the well-known TV presenter. 'She has head and neck cancer?' Her voice came out as a squeak, even though she was trying to be as professional as possible. News like that usually spread like wildfire and she was surprised she hadn't heard a thing.

Iain gave a curt nod. 'I'll talk you through it later. Now, go and eat.'

One of the theatre nurses gestured towards the door and held it open for her as she walked towards it. 'Come with me. I'll show you where you can grab a coffee. We'll have to be quick, mind. Iain will be starting again within ten minutes.'

Lexi followed her quickly to the nearby kitchen. This would be an ideal time to see how much she could find out about Iain from his colleagues.

She hadn't really met many of the staff from Kate's before.

She gave a grateful smile as the nurse poured out some coffee and handed her a cup. 'Take some biscuits. They're on the table. It's a free for all in here.'

Lexi smiled. 'Thanks for that. Have you worked with Iain long?'

The nurse lifted her eyebrows. 'Happy Harry?'

Lexi nearly choked. 'Is that what you call him?'

The nurse laughed. 'Actually, he's not the worst. Leo Hunter used to be much more grumpy but since he's met Lizzie he's all smiles. His brother Ethan seems to have taken on the mantle of biggest bear.' She walked over to the table and sat down next to Lexi. 'But to be fair to him he's still not recovered and he works far too long hours—they all do—but Ethan's trouble is he's far too stubborn to use his stick.'

Lexi frowned. 'I've never seen Ethan walking with a stick.'

'Exactly. I've worked in orthopaedic theatres

for too many years not to know when someone should be using a stick.'

Lexi pressed her lips together. It was time for a subject change, but the nurse was already back on her feet and washing her cup. No one got to hang around for long here. 'Let's go, Lexi.' She gave her a quick wink. 'Let's not keep our Scots laird waiting.'

Lexi followed her pale green scrubs out the door. Iain was near the end of scrubbing and his premiership footballer was being wheeled in the door. She almost couldn't believe the range of operations that Iain was involved in.

The surgery on the footballer player took several hours and her legs were already beginning to ache by the time a very nervous-looking Carol Kennedy was wheeled in. It was obvious she recognised Lexi immediately, and if she was surprised to see her she didn't show it. Instead, she gestured to her to come over.

Lexi's stomach was churning. She'd met Carol at numerous charity events over the years and had always found her to be as charming in person as she was on television. She reached over and gave Carol's hand a little squeeze. 'I'm so sorry to see you here, Carol.'

Carol nodded nervously, tears pooling in her eyes. 'Iain spoke to me beforehand about the filming. It's fine with me. I'll have some time to explain to the children when I go home.'

'Are you sure, Carol? The last thing I want to do is invade your privacy. If this is something you want kept out of the media, I completely understand. You know that my lips are sealed and I'll never breathe a word.'

Carol nodded gratefully. 'I appreciate that, Lexi. I've been fighting this cancer in private for quite some time. But after the surgery today I'll have some scars. Iain will do whatever he can, but I will have some scars around my neck that I don't want to have to spend my life telling lies about.' She shook her head. 'In a few days' time I'll be home and will have told my children. If filming the surgery helps other people and helps raise the profile of the clinic for the charities, it's fine with me.'

Carol gave a little nod as the anaesthetist signalled to her to lie back against the pillow. Lexi gave a final squeeze of her hand as the anaesthetist started slowing injecting the milky substance into her vein. A few seconds later Carol's body relaxed and her breathing was assisted. Lexi watched as Carol's head was tilted backwards but instead of sliding a tube down Carol's throat, as she'd expected, the anaesthetist slid a tube down her nose.

Iain saw the expression on her face. 'When we're doing surgery on the head and neck we often use nasotracheal intubation. It means we can maintain the patient's airway but still have access to do surgery in and around the face, mouth and neck.'

Lexi nodded. It made sense. If Iain needed access to the inside of Carol's mouth, it would be virtually impossible if a tube was down her throat.

'So what are you going to do for Carol?'

There was something so strange about seeing someone she knew lying on the operating table. Even though she'd recognised the footballer from earlier, she'd never met him before in person.

Iain and his team were positioning themselves around the table, a wide variety of surgical instruments around them. Even though Iain's mask was in place and all she could see were his brown eyes, his thick Scottish accent carried clearly across the theatre. 'All head and neck cancers are different. The extent of the surgery depends on the size of the cancer and where it is. If it's a small cancer of the mouth, there is often no scarring. But if the cancer has spread from the head or neck, the most likely place for it to go to is the lymph nodes in the neck—that's what has happened in Carol's case.'

It sounded so ominous when he said it like that. She couldn't bring herself to ask the obvious question. If this cancer was curable.

Iain was pointing inside Carol's mouth. 'I'm going to do to two types of surgery on Carol today. Transoral laser surgery is used to treat smaller cancers on the lip, mouth or throat. The laser removes the tumour using a high-power beam of light. The light is attached to a microscope so that I can see the tissue in detail when I'm operating. Carol's tumour is near the back of her throat near her larynx. We need to be very careful and precise. Anything we do could affect her speech. Once we've dealt with that tumour we need to deal with the spread.

'Neck dissection is necessary to remove all the affected lymph nodes in both sides of the neck. Tests have shown the cancer has spread to both sides. The nerve that helps move the lower lip can sometimes be affected. This can cause weakness on one side of the mouth and could potentially make her smile crooked. It would usually return to normal after a few months but I want to avoid that for Carol if I can.'

Lexi nodded. He was thinking about his patient and the impact this surgery could have on her livelihood. If Carol had problems with her speech, it would affect her ability to do her job. Things would be hard enough with her scarring. She didn't need any further complications.

She watched as the team draped Carol's skin and cleaned it prior to any incision. Iain attached the light and microscope to his visor and positioned himself at the entrance to her mouth. He gave his registrar, who was assisting, a nod and then looked around the theatre. 'People, I don't need to tell you how important my concentration is right now. No noise. No interruptions.'

For the next twenty minutes Lexi was scared to breathe. The theatre was eerily quiet. Occasionally Iain spoke quietly to his registrar and they adjusted their positions. She could see the intense focus of the laser. It was almost unthinkable that the slightest movement could mean the laser hitting healthy tissue instead of the tumour.

How could the theatre staff remain so calm? How could Iain keep his nerves in check? She felt sick just thinking about it, and from the look of her cameraman, he felt exactly the same.

Eventually Iain lifted his head, gave a nod and removed his head and eye set. He leaned back as far as he could, his back giving a painful crick.

Even beneath his mask she could see the corners of his eyes lift as he smiled. 'That's it, folks. You can talk again. We'll move on to the next part of the surgery.' The sigh of relief around the room was audible. Tense shoulders sagged and bad jokes started to circulate around the room again.

But Iain was in no way finished. He was joined at one point by Carol's cancer specialist and the two of them reviewed the earlier CT scan to ensure Iain would capture all the lymph nodes affected. The surgery was painstaking. Iain was more exacting, more precise than she could have ever have imagined. The surgery that had been expected to take four hours actually took six, all because Iain was determined not only to remove every possible trace of cancer but also to give Carol the best cosmetic outcome possible.

When he finally finished he inserted a small plastic drain on either side of her neck. After the care and attention to detail Lexi was surprised. It seemed almost unsightly. Iain caught her expression and gave a little shake of his head. 'We'll need to keep these in place for the next twenty-four hours to help drain any excess fluid. It will give Carol a better result overall, even though it doesn't look too pretty right now.'

He gave a final nod at the anaesthetist. 'All yours, Tony. Let's get some analgesia in and bring Carol round. I'll be around for the next two hours if you have any concerns.' He peeled off his gloves and mask. 'Thank you, everyone, for your hard work and attention to detail today. Let's do it all again on Thursday.'

It was almost as if his words gave her permission to sag against the wall. She'd found the day long, tiring, even though she'd been standing virtually in one spot. And this was just one day out of her life. Iain did this most days—sometimes every day—as well as seeing patients at the Hunter Clinic. No wonder he fell asleep in the office.

She watched as Iain moved back over to the theatre sinks to wash up. She could see the way the thin navy scrubs clung to every muscle, every sinew of his lithe body. He was chatting away to one of the scrub nurses as she cleaned the theatre around him. Not flirting. Just easy banter, the way they must act every day.

He was more relaxed in here than he was at the Hunter Clinic. And it didn't take her long to realise why. This was home for Iain. This was his comfort zone.

Iain wasn't renowned for his charm or easygoing manner. Quite the opposite, in fact. He was known for being gruff, sometimes downright blunt with colleagues and occasionally with patients. But his surgery spoke for itself. As did his patient recovery stories. No one could argue with those.

But if she wanted to increase publicity for the Hunter Clinic she was going to have to dig beneath the surface a little. Reveal a little of what she'd seen in Theatre today. The question was— how to do that? Iain was fiercely private and she was going to have to persuade him to lower his barriers just a touch to let their patients see the human side of the brilliant surgeon.

With the filming today she'd had a clear demonstration of his surgical skills and his commitment to the task. They'd even managed to capture some of his lighter moments with the theatre staff. All of this would be pure television gold, if only she could capture a little of the man as well.

She arched her back, just as he had done earlier. It didn't make the same alarming cricking noise but it certainly stretched her aching muscles. She dragged her eyes away from Iain. From the shaggy hair that had been released from the theatre cap. The hair that she was imagining running her fingers through.

This would never do. She was a professional.

She was always a professional. She'd met numerous celebrities throughout her life and very few of them had impressed her. Very few of them had made her imagination run wild. Not like the way it was at the moment. It must just be fatigue. She was tired—that was all. She'd had a late night last night, after dropping Iain home, and then an early start again this morning. It couldn't be anything else, could it?

She pushed open the door to the changing room and stripped off her pink scrubs and jumped into the shower. It only took a few minutes for the cool water to wake her up a little and she pulled on her red business suit and untied her hair, turning her head upside and down and giving it a good shake. After being confined up all day in a theatre cap, it felt good to finally have it loose again. Last she took her perfume from her bag and squirted liberally, finishing with her red lipstick.

There. Barely human again after how long? She checked her watch. Nearly twelve hours. Her stomach gave a loud rumble.

She was starving. And getting food—preferably of the unhealthy kind—was first on her list.

Iain was waiting at the changing-room doors, hoping he hadn't missed her. Lexi Robbins had been on his radar all day. It was the first time anyone had been in his operating theatre who had actually threatened his focus.

Iain McKenzie was a surgeon who slid into 'the zone' whenever he operated. The patient was his absolute focus—and nothing else penetrated.

But today had been a little different. Even though his focus had still been on his patients, for the first time he'd been conscious of his peripheral vision. The set of pale pink scrubs and wide blue eyes that had occasionally caught his attention.

It had been like a constant, persistent itch. And in Iain's mind the only way to deal with an itch was to scratch it. Maybe if he bent just a little and gave Lexi the interview she wanted she would move on to the next person on her hit list and he could return to a little sanity.

He smelt her first. Her scent permeating through the female changing-room doors. Seconds later the door opened and Lexi, a vision in red with her blonde hair tumbling around her shoulders, appeared.

He hesitated for a second. Lexi Robbins might have spent the day hidden in shapeless scrubs with her hair tucked away and no make-up on, but half an hour later the transformation into gorgeous sex princess was complete.

'Oh, Iain. I wasn't expecting to see you again. Is something wrong? Is Carol okay?'

He smiled. It was nice that her first thought was for the patient that she knew. He nodded his head. 'Carol is doing fine. I'm happy to leave her for the evening and check on her again in the morning. I think she'll have a comfortable night. Tomorrow we'll get her drains out and her husband will bring her kids in for a visit. A few days' rest with staff who will take good care of her will do her the world of good.'

Lexi's face brightened, the smile reaching from ear to ear. It was obvious her concern was genuine and he liked that about her.

'So what can I do for you, Iain? I thought you would be exhausted and want to get home.'

'I do. I mean, I would. But I'd like to get our interview over with first.'

'Really? After the day you've had?' She seemed genuinely surprised.

He nodded. 'Is that OK? Can we do it now?'

She seemed momentarily stunned then she reached into her bag to fumble with her phone. She pulled it out and stared at it for a second.

'Something wrong?'

She shrugged. 'Just the usual. Seventeen messages, I'll get to them later.' She looked around. 'John, the cameraman, will still be about. I'll send him a quick text. Is there somewhere around here we can set up?'

He pointed down the corridor. 'I've already sorted it. The staff at the Hunter Clinic have the use of some office space here. We can use a room just down the corridor.'

'Perfect.' She pressed the details into her

phone, sent the message to John and followed him down the corridor.

The office space was standard for any hospital. Not particularly big, with a desk, a phone and a chair. But the pièce de résistance was a picture window with a stunning backdrop of the Thames. Iain watched the expression on her face as she knew instantly it was the ideal setting for the interview. Not only did it give a really traditional view of London, it let patients know the setting for their potential hospital stay if they used the Hunter Clinic. What better selling point could there be?

He should have mentioned it to her earlier, but it hadn't even crossed his mind until his registrar had realised he was going to be interviewed and mentioned the spectacular view.

Lexi started pulling a chair over to the window, nodding at John as he appeared with his camera and instantly began setting up. 'The light will fade soon. We'd better be quick.'

Lexi, ever the professional, nodded and pulled out her notebook. She gave Iain a cheeky wink.

'Want me to sort out some make-up for you before your big screen debut?'

He laughed. 'I think I'll stick with the natural look.'

'And the scrubs?' She pointed to his navy scrubs. He hadn't even given them a second thought. For the sake of the clinic Lexi would probably have preferred him polished and scrubbed in his business suit. More associated with a Harley Street clinic. But that wasn't for Iain.

He lifted his hands. 'I'd prefer it if patients see me the way that I spend most of my day. They don't expect me to operate with the business suit on.'

She nodded. 'True. But I might need you to put on a business suit for some publicity shots later. Deal?' She lifted her eyebrows as her cheeky smile got even wider. 'Or how about a kilt, Iain? Because once the ladies have heard that Scottish accent...'

He lifted his hand. 'Enough. I might agree to the suit, but that's it.'

She sat down and waited for the signal from

John to say that he was ready. 'How about we negotiate on the kilt?'

He tried not to laugh. Did she have any idea how appealing she looked right now? With her designer red suit, black stilettos and red lipstick? Lexi Robbins didn't look like a girl who'd just spent the last twelve hours on her feet. Especially with those loose waves of blonde hair and sultry perfume floating in the air.

'I've negotiated on the interview. That's enough for now.'

John gave Lexi the nod and the light came on at the top of the camera. Iain adjusted his position under its glare.

'Let's start simply,' Lexi said. 'Start by telling us your name, what you do at Hunter Clinic and how long you've worked there.'

Iain nodded and took a deep breath. If he could get this over and done with tonight then this could be the end of his contact with Lexi Robbins.

This itch just didn't need scratched. It was like a chicken pox. It needed the head knocked clean off it.

He looked towards the camera. Smiling just wasn't his natural instinct. 'I'm Iain McKenzie and you might guess by the accent that I'm from Edinburgh. I've worked at the Hunter Clinic for the last two years, specialising in reconstructive surgery.'

Lexi nodded. 'Iain, can you tell us the difference between general plastic surgery and reconstructive surgery?'

He nodded curtly, trying to choose his words carefully. Trying to use terms that people would be familiar with instead of medical jargon. 'I can do all the things that a general plastic surgeon can do—face lifts, tummy tucks, breast enhancements—but I specialise in surgery that's a bit more complicated. For example, lots of my patients have had surgery in other places—other countries—that might not have given them the outcome they wanted or expected. Some of the surgery I do would be termed corrective surgery.'

Lexi made some circling motions with her hand, urging him to continue.

He took a deep breath. 'I also deal with a number of patients who've had cancer that's affected various parts of their bodies. That can be anywhere, their breasts, their faces, head and neck. All areas that might require reconstruction after the cancer has been removed and treatment has been completed. Often these surgeries require rebuilding, reshaping or prosthetic implants to give the patient back the body that they want.'

'Is it purely cosmetic reconstructive surgery that you do at the Hunter Clinic, Iain?'

He shook his head. 'I also specialise in functional surgery. I've treated a number of patients with oral and cleft-palate defects. In this country, most children would have surgery done at a young age. The same facilities aren't available in all countries and I've dealt with a number of adult patients who've come to the Hunter Clinic to have these corrected later in life. It can make a huge difference to their ability to eat and to their speech to have these corrected later in life.

'Of course, we also have a number of rehabilitation services, such as speech therapists and dieticians, available to support the care of these patients. All our services are about giving people the best possible outcome from their surgeries.' He shook his head firmly. 'I wouldn't perform any surgery that I didn't believe would have a positive impact on the patient.'

He was trying his absolute best not to say anything that would make Lexi throw her hands up in horror. He didn't want to have to repeat this interview over and over again because he'd been way too blunt about some of the vanity-driven requests of clients.

Lexi shifted in her chair, crossing her legs and giving him an unexpectedly good view of her shapely calves and thighs.

'That's great, Iain, thanks. Now, can you tell us a little more about yourself?'

She was staring at him with those big blue eyes. Smiling, with her open face and manner. He could almost forget that the camera was in the room with them.

'Well, there's not much to tell. I grew up in Edinburgh, Scotland. I did my university and medical training at hospitals in Edinburgh. I was a Scout—though not a very good one. I could never master the art of lighting a fire.' He raised his eyebrows at Lexi, who let out a little laugh.

'Our patients would like to know a little more about the man behind the surgeon's mask. How about I ask you some questions?'

He shifted in his chair a little uncomfortably. From this position it was still too easy to keep his eyes on Lexi's legs.

She leaned forward a little, as if she was trying to encourage him. It also gave him the slightest hint of her cleavage down her firmly fastened white blouse. Cleavage that he would love to get his hands on—to see who had done her surgery and whether it met with his approval. To see whether it was right for Lexi.

Those legs again and the thoughts of having his hands on her breasts was causing a familiar sensation. One that a camera certainly shouldn't see. He shifted his position.

'Let's try some quick-fire questions.'

'Yes, let's.' The words came out almost unconsciously. It must be fatigue. That must be why he was being so pliable. That, or the fact he needed to try some distraction techniques right now. Normally, by this point he would have got up and walked away. Personal questions really went against all his principles.

'Movies—action or drama?'

He shook his head. 'Neither. Sci-fi. Every single time.' These kinds of question were fine. They were harmless. Inane.

'Italian, Chinese or Indian food?'

'Depends entirely what day of the week it is—and, what I'm doing the next day. Italian, with no garlic, if I'm operating the next day. Chinese if it's heading towards a weekend. And Indian food on a Saturday night, preferably with a pint.'

'A pint?'

'You know.' He lifted and gestured with his wrist. 'Like all good Scotsmen. A pint of beer.'

She smiled again. 'Just the one?'

He shrugged. 'Normally, depends on the company.'

She paused, as if taking in those words, then glanced back down at her notes. 'Best job—apart from the Hunter Clinic, of course.'

He frowned, racking his brain. 'There are two—completely different from each other. One, as a trainee I spent two months with the mountain rescue team in the Swiss Alps. Learnt more in those two months than I did at any other point in my training. It was fabulous.'

Lexi nodded. 'And the second?'

'Voluntary work. I visited one of the Romanian orphanages a number of years ago and did some of the specialist cleft-lip and palate surgeries that I described earlier.' His voice lowered. 'It was a real eye-opener. And a really rewarding time. I'm planning on going back next summer.'

Lexi was looking excited. 'The Hunter Clinic will be supporting some charity work and has just joined up with Olivia Fairchild's charity Fair Go. Will you be available to do some work for that charity, Iain?'

The way she said the words was so innocent. So off the cuff. But he knew fine well she was capturing him on tape. Just as well he'd already had this conversation with Leo Hunter and had agreed to help in any way he could. 'I'm happy to help the Hunter Clinic in any charity that they choose to support—just as they are happy to

help me, in any charity I choose to support.'
Touché. These things worked both ways.

Lexi was still leaning forward. Still making
him feel as if it were only the two of them in
the room. It was starting to fire his imagination
again. Make him remember the things that had
kept him from sleeping last night.

She gave him her dazzling smile. 'What about
your favourite holiday?'

It was an innocent question. A completely in-
nocuous question. But for Iain it hit a nerve he
was unprepared for. Pictures were instantly con-
jured up in his mind. Pictures of a perfect honeymoon in Venice, with thousands of images
of the multicoloured houses, the islands, the
canals, the gondolas and the wonders of St
Mark's Square. If he breathed in deeply enough
he could practically smell the place. The words
formed on his lips without him even thinking.
'Venice, for my honeymoon. It was beautiful.
The most perfect city in the world.'

'You were married?'

The surprised tone in Lexi's voice brought him
to his senses. He knew he should answer this ca-

sually. It had been a slip. His fault, something he didn't normally reveal, and he could have kicked himself for saying the words out loud.

But there was something else. Something hanging in the air between them. Something that he hadn't quite yet managed to fathom.

And as Lexi sat there in the dimming light, with her wide blue eyes, designer red suit and long, lithe limbs, all he could remember was the Lexi from his dream last night. The one who had been straddling him with those long legs. The one who had danced those red lips across his forehead and chest. Taking him to a whole place he hadn't visited in a long time.

His reaction was automatic. He stood up, causing both Lexi and John to start in their positions. Trying to erase all those thoughts from his head and trying to push the aroma of her perfume from his senses.

He needed to get out of there. He needed space. More importantly, he needed to get away from *her*. As far away as possible.

'Iain? Iain, what's wrong?' She stood up,

straightening her skirt and taking a step towards him.

He couldn't let her touch him. He couldn't let her be near him at all right now.

'Interview over,' he growled as he strode to the door and flung it open, letting it slam off the wall as his steps ate up the corridor outside.

CHAPTER FIVE

'AS IF THIS day could get any worse.' Lexi let out a sigh as the buzzer sounded loudly again. It was almost as if someone upstairs was laughing at her, waiting until her toe was perfectly poised above the millions of lavender-scented bubbles and her satin dressing gown had just hit the floor.

The buzzing was becoming more incessant, more desperate. So she picked the dressing-gown back off the floor and knotted it tightly around her waist. 'This had better be good,' she muttered as she made her way to the door.

She swung the door open, fatigue stopping her from putting her sensible head in place. The one that would make her put all her locks in place and check through the peephole before opening the door, half-dressed.

'Iain!'

The very last person she had expected to see tonight.

The cool night air swept around her thin dressing-gown, making it billow against her legs. She tried to grab it, tried to hide the swathes of skin it was threatening to expose.

Iain was leaning against her doorjamb, his shaggy hair looking as if he'd spent the last two hours running his fingers through it.

Twenty minutes. That was how long the interview had lasted. And while what she'd captured initially was just what she'd hoped for and would be perfect for the publicity campaign, the ending had been more than a little abrupt.

She'd been left standing with her jaw bouncing off the floor as John had shrugged, packed up his camera and left for the night. Iain had vanished. No one in the hospital had known where he was and Lexi had been left to make her way home wondering what on earth she'd done wrong.

A long hot bubble bath, a glass of wine and a mountain of pizza had been on the cards.

'Can I come in?' His manner was still abrupt

but he was looking at her with those big brown eyes that sucked you in and made you forget how to give appropriate answers. It didn't help that every hair on her skin was standing on end and she couldn't bear to look down and see the effects on her nipples.

She stood aside. 'If you want,' she muttered, unsure whether this was a good idea or not.

Iain walked into her flat, instantly filling it with his large frame. It wasn't as if she lived somewhere small. By most people's proportions Lexi's London flat was positively comfortable. But just having Iain in it seemed to make the air close in around her. She was feeling completely and utterly underdressed.

He was pacing. Pacing around her flat. He had the obligatory grey suit on, with a dark blue shirt, his top button open and tie askew. 'Look, Lexi, about earlier—'

'What about earlier?' she interrupted, folding her arms across her chest as it seemed the safest position for them.

He stopped pacing and took a step towards her,

closing the space between them in an instant. His voice was low. 'I'm not very good at this.'

'Not very good at what?' Was that her voice that sounded all squeaky? How embarrassing. He was too close. She could reach right out and put her hand on the plane of his chest. *So not a good idea.* It was better to keep her eyes fixed on her dark wooden floor and bare feet with their painted toenails.

She heard him sigh. 'Saying sorry.'

Her head snapped back up in time to see him run his fingers through his hair and fix his brown eyes on hers. So not what she was expecting.

Being this close to Iain McKenzie was more than a little disconcerting. Particularly when she was partially dressed.

'Lexi?' he said softly.

'What?'

'Would you mind putting some clothes on? It's kind of distracting, seeing you like this.'

She felt the colour rush into her cheeks. On one hand she should be glad that he found her distracting—on the other? She wasn't entirely sure if that was a good or a bad thing.

'I was just about to step into the bath,' she said by way of explanation.

'Have you eaten?' He glanced at the clock.

She shook her head. 'Ordering pizza was next on my list.'

He reached over and touched her arm, his warm hand circling her cold wrist. 'Then let me take you out to dinner.'

She pulled back a little, trying not to focus on the electricity shooting up her arm. 'It's nearly nine o'clock. Where are you going to find somewhere that still has a table?'

He gave her a knowing smile and tapped the edge of his nose. 'Leave that to me. Will you come, Lexi? We need to talk.'

For a second she hesitated. Was this a good idea? Maybe she could persuade Iain McKenzie that the job she was doing was actually a worthwhile one. Maybe she could persuade him to be a little more involved. Anything that would help the charity work of the clinic would surely be worth a dinner. No matter how blunt her dinner partner was.

She looked down at her pink toes. 'What do I need to wear?'

'You could wear a plastic bin bag, Lexi, you'd still look good.' The words tripped off his tongue as easily as could be. He didn't even seem embarrassed by them.

She walked off towards the bedroom. 'That didn't help!' she shouted over her shoulder.

Fifteen minutes later he walked her down a street in London she'd never visited before. A warm and enveloping smell started to surround them as Iain walked towards a red-painted door and pushed it open. There was no traditional restaurant window looking out onto the street and advertising its presence. Instead there was a winding staircase up to what felt like the top of a private townhouse.

The smell was intriguing her. 'What is this place?' She looked around for a restaurant name or menu but there was nothing obvious.

A man appeared at Iain's side and pulled a curtain aside for them, revealing a small intimate restaurant. 'Nice to see you again, mate. Find yourself a table.'

She smiled at the rich Australian accent and informality of it all. The restaurant was busy, with only a few free tables.

Then reality started to hit and she took a little step backwards. 'Isn't that Georgie Perkins, the Oscar-winning actress?' The woman was dressed in a green suit and drinking wine with her husband and another couple.

Iain gave a nod and pulled out a chair for her. Lexi smoothed the front of her red jersey dress as she sat down, yet again feeling instantly underdressed.

'Hey, Iain.'

'Hey, Kevin, nice to see you.' He gave the man on their right a curt nod.

Lexi leaned forward and gritted her teeth. 'Sir Kevin Bain? Chairman of the richest football club in the country?'

Iain reached over and grabbed some bread out of the basket sitting on the table. 'Yup, him and wife number three.' He leaned forward and winked. 'She's one of ours, you know.'

'What is this place?' Lexi asked, looking around and realising she still hadn't seen a name anywhere.

'It's Frank's,' he said simply.

'And who is Frank?' she asked. 'And how come I've never heard of this place?' She pointed over at the other diners. 'Other people obviously have.'

'Take it from me, this place is for good eating and good wine. You won't find any paparazzi hanging around outside the door, and it never needs to advertise.'

Lexi settled back into her chair. He was right. The place had a certain ambience about it, as if the celebrities who were there knew their privacy would be guarded. She had dined around lots of people like this, but she'd never seen them quite so relaxed—quite so unguarded. Would the same rules apply to Iain? Was this why he'd brought her here?

The guy from the door appeared and handed them menus. He looked at Lexi and held out his hand. 'I haven't met you before, have I?'

She shook her head and met his firm hand-shake. 'Lexi Robbins. I work with Iain.'

'Lucky man. I'm Frank. If it's not on the menu—just ask and I'll make it for you. I can handle all the allergy quirks, all the special diets, but if you're a crazy who just doesn't want any calories then I'll pour you a glass of water and charge you a hundred bucks.'

She laughed, instantly liking the big Australian, then grabbed her stomach as it let out a little grumble.

He looked skyward. 'My favourite noise in the world. What will it be, lady?'

Lexi handed him back the menu. She'd barely even glanced at it but felt as if she could trust his judgement. 'I'm a chicken girl. Do anything you like with it—except give me bones.'

Frank blew some of his hair off his forehead. 'Amateur!' He turned to Iain, 'Go on, master of the universe. Surprise me.'

Iain rolled his eyes. 'If you keep talking to me like that, I won't come back.'

'Fat chance.'

He nodded and handed over his menu. 'You're right. I'll have the usual.'

Frank disappeared muttering, only to reappear and plonk a bottle of red wine on the table along with a couple of glasses.

Iain lifted the bottle and gave a smile. 'Are you okay with red, or would you prefer something else?'

She lifted her glass towards him. 'Red's fine. Just not too much.'

Iain filled her glass part way then did the same with his own.

'To Frank's?'

She smiled and clinked glasses with him. 'To Frank's. Here's hoping the food is as good as you promised.'

Iain nodded with confidence. 'You've nothing to worry about here.' He looked around at their surroundings. 'This place is all about chilling and relaxing. That's why I brought you here. We could have gone to Drake's but the food, and the company, are infinitely better here.'

She smiled. Drake's would be packed to the rafters right now—probably with most of the staff from the Hunter Clinic and St Catherine's. It was unlikely they would have managed to have any kind of conversation in there.

'Who is Frank?'

'Just a sad Australian who needed an op one day. He told me he owned a restaurant and invited me for dinner after that.'

'You're not going to reveal?'

He shook his head. 'Only if you get me drunk.'

There it was. That little hint of humour that appeared on the rarest of occasions. She liked it. It proved that the gruff exterior of Iain McKenzie wasn't as rock solid as it first seemed and the man could actually laugh at himself.

He set his glass on the table. 'So, Lexi Robbins. I'm curious about you.'

'Why?'

'Because I don't know much about you.'

She sighed. 'Haven't you ever read a newspaper or a gossip magazine? My life's been pretty much an open book since the second I was born.'

'Yeah, but that's not the kind of thing I want to know.'

She leaned forward a little. 'So what do you want to know, Iain McKenzie?'

She hadn't meant it to come out that way. Slightly flirtatious. Slightly coy. But they were sitting in a darkened candlelit restaurant in the middle of London after a stressful day. She really didn't want to have to think too hard. She was only doing what came naturally.

His eyes skimmed over her. She could feel them. Taking in her loose curls and comfortably fitted dress. She hadn't bothered with much make-up, only reapplying her lipstick and adding some mascara.

His finger ran round the rim of his glass. 'I'm curious why Leo Hunter hired you to be the head of PR. You must be good—you must be very good, because everyone working at the clinic was handpicked by Leo.'

'And the implication is that I don't seem that good?' Her reaction was instant. She could get angry. She could get upset and tearful. But to be frank she'd heard it all before and was far too tired to fight. She leaned back in her seat and took a sip of her wine.

'I didn't say that.' His voice was quiet. Controlled. As if he was trying to get the measure of her.

She let out a sigh. 'You didn't have to, Iain. A million others have implied it before you.'

His eyebrow rose ever so slightly. 'Why would they do that?'

She took another sip of wine. It was official. A few sips were definitely hitting the right spot and relaxing her. That's what happened when you hardly managed to eat all day.

'Let's start at the very beginning. You might have guessed I was a bit of an accessory to my parents.'

'That seems a bit harsh.'

She let out a snort. 'Try living it. It gets a bit much when they constantly tell you you're not pretty enough or good enough.'

Iain leaned forward, his eyes practically smoking. 'Your parents did that?'

She shook her head a little. 'Not in so many words. It was implied—in a lot of ways. I was constantly in the press, being compared to my mother, the supermodel. What girl really wants to spend her life being told she's not as pretty as her mother?' Lexi lowered her eyes. 'I focused on other things. I was academic. I liked school, I guess in that respect I took after my father. Then I had a bit of an accident and I was out of school for a while.'

'What happened?' She could see the concern on his face and felt a lump forming in her throat. So much time had passed. It had been so long ago. She'd got over this and put it behind her, she didn't feel the need to go into details.

'I had a horse-riding accident and needed some major surgery.' It was best to leave the specifics out. 'My mum and dad were there for a few days, but they were busy. They both had contractual obligations. So once they knew I would live but need some serious recuperation, they handed me over to my Aunt Jo.'

Iain wrinkled his nose. 'I thought you said your family was permanently in the papers. I've not heard of your Aunt Jo.'

Lexi smiled. 'I bet you have. Josephine Kirk. She's my father's sister.'

His eyes widened. 'Wasn't she an ambassador for children for the UN?'

Lexi nodded. 'After I recovered from surgery I still wasn't really fit for school. I spent the summer with Aunt Jo—and almost every summer after that. We're close.'

'Closer than you are to your mum and dad?'

'Absolutely.' There was no hesitation in the word.

Iain sucked in his breath. He had a great relationship with his mum and dad. They'd been his absolute backbone when he'd lost his wife. He couldn't imagine not knowing that they would always be there for him. Lexi had described herself as an 'accessory'—what kind of parents did she have?

He watched her in the flickering candlelight. She seemed totally at ease, totally oblivious to the casual, admiring glances she was receiving. He'd never given Lexi much thought. Even when she'd started working at the clinic he hadn't really taken much notice of her credentials or her work ethic. But she was rapidly turning into the most interesting woman he'd met in a long time.

* * *

Lexi was tempted to fill the silence. Should she tell Iain more?

He was a doctor. He would understand.

But she wasn't really ready to share any personal details. Her aunt was the wisest woman she'd known. Lexi's surgery had been extensive—a horseshoe in her lower abdomen had caused tremendous damage to her young body, meaning that she would never be able to have children of her own. But her aunt had taken her to a place to show her the little children in this world who would need someone like her—someone to love and care for them in future years.

And it had helped Lexi move on. To stop thinking about the fact she'd never be pregnant and give birth, but to realise that not everyone became a mother in the same way. To realise that if her dream was to have a family then the possibility was there.

Very few people knew that detail about her. And even though Iain was watching her with those big chocolate-brown eyes, lulling her into a false sense of security that might make her reveal her innermost secrets, she just couldn't say anything else.

This was about protecting herself and protecting the decisions that she made. She'd learned from her mistakes. So no matter what spark she currently felt towards the sexy Scot, it wouldn't make her reveal her most intimate secrets.

'Here we go, folks. Chicken with no bones, and my own special concoction, and the usual for you.' Frank placed the plates down on the table with a flourish and then melted into the back ground once again.

Lexi leaned forward and breathed deeply. 'Oh, this smells great. I'm starved. What have you got?'

Iain smiled. 'Pulled pork with spicy sauce and hand-cut chips. Can't beat it. It's perfect every time I come here.' He picked up his knife and fork. 'What did Frank make for you?'

Lexi smiled. 'I think he secretly switched on his telepathic powers and invaded my brain. He's given me something that I'll love, chicken with mushrooms and some spicy potato bravas. I can't wait.'

Iain nodded. 'Frank always seems to get it just right.' He waved his fork at her. 'Dig in.'

She did. And Iain watched with enjoyment as she cleared her plate and then sat back and gave a sigh. 'That was much better than pizza.'

A woman who wasn't scared to eat. What a relief. At least fifty per cent of the women he saw at the Hunter Clinic had some weird ideas about diets and eating. Some of them were even refused surgery because their BMIs were so low it made them anaesthetic risks. It was nice to be in the company of a woman who seemed comfortable in her own skin.

The strange thing was, it obviously hadn't always been the case. She'd already told him about her experiences of being compared to her mother, and there was the fact she'd obviously had implants. Why would someone like Lexi think she needed to have surgery?

But the more time he spent in her company the more he was drawn to her. She was warm and charming with a good sense of humour. And even though she'd spent part of her life in the spotlight she certainly wasn't the vacant blonde she was sometimes portrayed as in the press.

Lexi was highly intelligent, well read with an opinion on everything. And pushing aside the breasts and fabulous legs, there was just more and more to like about her.

'What did your parents think about you doing your degree?'

She stared at him and the edges of her lips curled upwards. 'Why do I get the impression that you already know?'

'I'm just guessing your mother might have had other plans for you.'

'Oh, she did. And they all involved being her personal assistant and PR girl. She was most annoyed when I passed my exams with flying colours and got a place to study international business.'

Iain nodded slowly. 'Interesting choice.'

'It was fabulous. And in the final year you had a placement in a real business for six months. I loved it. They offered me a job straight after uni.'

'And did you take it?'

'I did for a few years.' She took another sip of

her wine. 'Funny thing was, I actually found myself drawn towards PR work. Maybe my mother knew me better than I knew myself all along.'

'So did you work for her?'

Lexi smiled. And it was the best smile of the evening, reaching all the way into her eyes and giving her a cheeky sparkle. 'Not a chance.'

He laughed. There were so many qualities here that he hadn't seen before. Hadn't taken the chance to see. All because from the second he'd set eyes on Lexi she'd woken up his libido like a shrieking alarm clock. Something he definitely hadn't been prepared for. And something he definitely hadn't been ready to acknowledge.

'So how did you end up being head-hunted by Leo Hunter at the clinic?'

She nodded. 'Leo is very persuasive. I was working for a variety of charities when he approached me. At first I wasn't interested in trying to raise the profile of a private clinic. It seemed almost the exact opposite of what I was currently doing. But Leo told me about the work they wanted to fund and the people he wanted to help by increasing the client base of the clinic…' Her voice tailed off and Iain smiled.

'I get it. Leo is very persuasive.'

She smiled again, her blue eyes fixed on his face. He pushed his wine glass aside. Lexi Robbins was beginning to wreak havoc on his senses.

'I like the clinic. I'm proud of the job I do. I want to be known for me, Lexi Robbins. I hate it when a newspaper article starts, "Lexi Robbins, daughter of…"' She shook her head. 'I'm my own person. But I'm also wise enough to know that some of the clients I've brought to the clinic saw me in the first instance because I'm my father's—or my mother's—daughter.'

Iain lifted his glass and held it up to her. 'Well, in that case I want to make a toast. To Lexi Robbins, PR genius of Hunter Clinic, who will bring in thousands of pounds to help fund the charity projects.'

She lifted her glass and gave him a wink. '*Tens* of thousands of pounds.'

They clinked glasses.

'Dessert?' Frank appeared at their side again,

clearing their dinner plates. 'Could I tempt you with a beautiful pear tart with chocolate sauce?'

Lexi shook her head. 'It sounds heavenly, Frank, but I'm all chickened out.'

'Too much?' he asked.

'No, just perfect. But I honestly couldn't eat another bite.' She glanced at her watch. 'It's been a long day and I'm feeling kind of tired.' She looked apologetically at Iain and he stood immediately to come to her side and pull her chair out.

'No problem at all.' He pulled some money from his wallet to pay Frank and gave him a wave as he helped Lexi on with her coat. It was late. He should have paid more attention to the time. Not everyone was an insomniac like him. Not everyone did anything possible rather than go to bed and stare at the ceiling, hoping to have a dreamless night.

'I hope you don't mind, Iain.' She spun round to face him and her big blue eyes and blonde curls were directly under his nose. Just inches away from him.

'Of course not, Lexi. I'll walk you home. I should have kept my eye on the time.' He held out his arm as they walked down the stairs and out onto the street and was secretly glad when she slid her arm through his.

He was telling himself he was only being polite. It didn't mean anything else. It didn't mean anything at all.

But walking through the darkened London streets with a beautiful woman on his arm gave him a little buzz. And not in the traditional sense. As a surgeon Iain knew better than most that true beauty came from the inside. And tonight he'd been well and truly exposed to the true beauty of Lexi Robbins.

He'd watched a programme once where people sat behind a screen and described how they looked to an artist who drew a picture of them from their description. Then one of their friends described them to the same artist. The programme ended with the pictures hanging side by side. It truly reflected that people often didn't see themselves the way others saw them. The pictures where the people had described themselves were nowhere near as beautiful as the ones where their friends had described them.

And the friends' pictures were a much more accurate reflection of the individual.

Why had this sprung to mind? Because he could tell—just from tonight and their conversation—that Lexi couldn't see the beauty he could, both inside and out.

It still intrigued him why she'd felt the need to get implants. But it seemed too personal a question to ask. It could be that Lexi had had other reasons for surgery and the implants were a consequence of that.

They rounded the corner into her street.

'You're awfully quiet, Iain. Something wrong?' Even her voice sounded merry. Lexi was a pleasure to be around.

'Not at all. I'm just enjoying the company.'

'That'll be a first. You're usually playing hide and seek with me.'

Yes. She was nobody's fool, even if she was usually too polite to say so. It seemed the wine had loosened her tongue.

He stopped and spun her round, catching her around the waist. 'Lexi Robbins, I have no idea what you mean,' he said in mock horror.

She pointed her finger at his wide chest. 'I'll have you know, Iain McKenzie, that I was the champion hide-and-seeker as a kid.' She lifted her hands in the air. 'You can run but you can't hide.'

'Who says I want to hide?' he said, closing the space between them in an instant and pulling her hard against his chest.

This time the sensation of her firm breasts wasn't a surprise. But the way her body melded into his was. It was almost as if she...fitted.

This time her hands rested on his shoulders. The initial flash of surprise disappeared from her eyes and her gaze remained steady on his.

Her voice was a little breathless. 'Admit it, Iain, you have been hiding from me.' There wasn't another person on the street. It was just the two of them. Nothing and no one to interrupt them.

'And all of a sudden I can't imagine why,' he said quietly.

Silence. The tension between them was almost palpable. The air was practically crackling.

Then she almost tipped him over the edge. Her

tongue ran along her red lips, moistening them and making them glisten in the dim light. Her voice was hoarse. 'Neither can I,' she whispered, as her fingers pressed into his shoulder bones.

He didn't think. He didn't stop to think for a second.

This was all about instinct. And his instinct was to make her his.

He bent his head, taking her lips as his own. Claiming them in every way possible. His hands pulled her hips close against his then he lifted them and wound them through her blonde hair. So soft, so silky between his fingers.

She let out a little gasp and raised herself up on tiptoe, trying to get herself even closer to him. Her hands left his shoulders and slid around to the back of his neck, curving themselves across the expanse of his back.

There was nothing tender and gentle about this kiss. This was pure and utter unbridled lust. That scent was under his nose again, drifting through his senses. It had followed him for days, driving him slowly and utterly crazy with the thoughts it evoked in his brain.

Lexi was matching him every step of the way. He pushed her back from the pavement towards the entrance of her flat. His hands were drifting under her coat, up the sensual curves of her waist and hips, relishing the feel of the clingy jersey dress beneath his fingertips. Then his hands met her breasts, the rational part of his brain wondering if she would react to his touch but the sensual part of his brain already on a mission he had to complete. Beneath the thin material her nipples reacted in his palms, making him stifle a groan in the back of his throat.

He pressed her further against the wall, one of her legs rising up and hitching on his hip, his hardness pushing against her core. His head had fallen to her neck now, to the source of that delicious sensual scent. He could taste it under his lips as his tongue moved around the soft skin at the bottom of her neck and along her fine clavicle. Her hands were moving in one direction—with a distinct purpose—and his back arched towards her.

His fingers were following suit, pushing up her dress and edging along the inside of her thigh.

'Iain,' she panted.

'What?' He didn't even look up, didn't want to stop what was happening.

Her body was reacting to his every touch, completely and utterly responding to every single move he made.

A cool breeze danced across his skin where she'd opened a few buttons on his shirt and the sweep of air caused him to stiffen.

He looked up. Lexi's gaze was fixed on his. Part of it passion, part of it confusion. He could see the wealth of emotions behind her blue eyes and it brought him crashing to earth with an almighty thump.

Lexi. It was Lexi Robbins standing in front of him now.

It was Lexi Robbins who had stoked his emotions so high he'd almost choked on them.

Blonde hair, blue eyes. Staring at him with a look of expectation, a look of reciprocation of the feelings that were bubbling inside him.

It was like a bucketful of ice chips tumbling

over his body. The horrible, stomach-churning realisation that not once this evening—not once—had he given Bonnie a second thought.

He stepped backwards, trying to put some distance between him and Lexi. Distance that had already formed in his mind a mile wide.

For the last few years he'd thought about Bonnie every single day. *Every single day.*

Whether it was first thing in the morning when he woke up, at some quiet time snatched in the middle of the day, or late at night when he was home alone, Bonnie had appeared in his thoughts every day. Sometimes the memories were good ones, happy thoughts of places they'd been, things they'd experienced together.

Other times he was in Theatre when he relived those horrendous moments. Losing his precious wife and losing his twins in one fell swoop.

Other times he was racked with guilt, replaying conversations when he'd persuaded her to give IVF one last go. To give that particular chance of having a family that way one last try.

So many steps in his life that he wanted to

rewind. Wanted to turn back the clock and do differently.

But no matter what the thoughts, no matter whether the memories were good or bad, they had been there. Every single day. Until now.

The guilt was horrendous. From the second he'd got up that morning he'd thought about Lexi, knowing that she was meeting him at Kate's.

He'd even thought about her at some points today during surgery. Unthinkable.

The only time today he'd given Bonnie any thought had been the tiniest fleeting moment at the end of the interview when he'd walked out.

But it had vanished in a flash when he'd realised his reaction had been over the top and his priority had been to apologise to Lexi. Not to sit down for a few seconds and wonder why he was so mixed up. Wonder why he was reacting in such an irrational way.

Somewhere along the way an invisible line had been crossed without him even realising it. A line that he'd drawn in the sand years ago to protect himself from taking actions that could affect the life of another. The consequences were too big a cross to bear.

Casual relationships were fine. But Lexi was no one's casual relationship. And he'd known that from the second he'd seen her and realised the affect she had on him.

Avoiding her had been a self-preservation technique—one he should have stuck to.

'Iain? Iain, what's wrong?' Her voice was still breathy, panting, as if she was full of pent-up frustration. The last thing he needed right now. What he needed right now was space. Distance. As much as possible.

'This was a mistake. A big mistake.' With every word he stepped back a little further, as if it helped him say the words.

A splash of rain landed on his nose and he looked upwards at the dark sky above him. Clouds were circling above his head in more ways than one.

'I have to go. I'm sorry, Lexi. Let's just leave it. Just leave it alone.'

She started to shake her head. Utter confusion was painted across her face and his gut clenched at the fact he'd hurt her. It had never been his intention. Things had just got out of control.

'But, Iain—'

He whipped away as the rain started to deluge the pavement around him, his stride lengthening with every step.

He didn't care about the weather, he didn't care about the rain.

He just needed to get away from her. Get away from her intoxicating scent. Even as he walked down the street he could still smell her—smell her perfume on his clothes.

He lifted his hand and something reflected under the orange streetlight. A strand of shiny blonde hair, glittering like a moonlit stream. She was everywhere.

Not just in his head.

Guilt ground away at him. He should be thinking of Bonnie and his lost children. He should be remembering the terrible impact he'd had on three lives, all because he'd persuaded his beautiful wife to give IVF one last try. She hadn't been sure. The previous two attempts had been tougher than either of them had anticipated, and they'd almost resigned themselves to the fact that they wouldn't have a family by a natural means.

And he'd felt fine about that.

So, why, why had he pushed for one last try? Even he couldn't fathom out the details now. The decision seemed so ridiculous, so misguided. And that had been before the eventual outcome.

Carrying two tiny white coffins next to his wife's had been the end of Iain McKenzie.

It had been the end of the light-hearted, laughter-filled man that he'd become thanks to Bonnie. She had always been the person to lift his sometimes dark moods. She'd always been the glass-half-full kind of girl.

She'd been his shining light. And look what he'd done to her.

'Beloved Wife. Beloved Son. Beloved Daughter.'

The words etched in gold on the black granite, along with the three red poppies, were forever in the back of his mind.

Maybe he'd been wrong to come to London. Maybe he should have stayed in Edinburgh, where he could have visited the grave every day?

But the smoky strands of depression had been circling around his brain. Creeping up on him with their strangulating hands. His parents, his friends and his family had all urged him to go with Leo. They had told him it was for the best. They had told him he needed a fresh start.

They hadn't counted on Lexi Robbins.

And, three years later, neither had he.

CHAPTER SIX

THE DEMONS WERE whispering in Lexi's ear again. Those horrible little voices of self-doubt and self-deprecation.

She'd fought hard to keep them at bay as it seemed as if there had been constant reinforcement of them in her life.

First from her parents. Then from her boyfriend. The one who'd liked her name and standing instead of Lexi Robbins the person, Lexi Robbins, the human being.

Jack Parker had spent most of his time mocking her bedroom performance and mocking her flat chest. It had taken her a long time to get the measure of him. And it had been at his insistence that she'd gone for the boob job.

Her hands went automatically to her breasts. Automatically to the over-sensitised skin that Iain McKenzie had just been touching.

The rain was pelting down, soaking straight through her thin raincoat and even thinner jersey dress. But Lexi didn't care about the rain.

She was feeling a surge of anger in her belly.

It had taken too long, too many years for her to come to terms with who she really was and not who people thought she should be. The gentle, steady support from her aunt had been invaluable. She wasn't about to stand back and let those old feelings invade her life again.

She was strong now. She was determined.

She leaned back against the wall as her legs gave way a little under the maelstrom of emotions that were threatening to overwhelm her.

She could see her ex's face in her mind. The super-confident Jack Parker squeezing her small breasts contemptuously and comparing them to the latest model in the newspaper. Telling her that she'd never look good in their holiday shots in the Bahamas. The ones that he'd tipped the newspapers off about.

And his caustic, consistent putdowns had chipped away at her already low self-esteem.

She had already worn two sets of chicken fillets in her bra. She hadn't particularly liked her body shape herself. Dresses that had fitted her around the hips and thighs had sagged over her chest—unless she'd worn her chicken fillets. But she could have lived with that because the rest of the world hadn't seen her naked.

Only Jack had. But he hadn't liked what he'd seen.

It had taken all her strength and resilience to get rid of him. Once she'd had the breast implants he'd started suggesting other improvements. So she'd made the ultimate improvement and got rid of him—tossing his clothes out onto the street—before he'd dragged her down any further.

She would never, ever let another man do that to her.

Let another man make her feel that way.

Not even Iain McKenzie.

It had taken her time to accept the changes to her body. To finally realise that she did actually like the shape she had now. She only wished she'd made the decision for herself. She wouldn't let anyone chip away at her self-esteem again.

She started to walk in the rain. Striding down the same street that he'd taken, following the road to his townhouse. She didn't care that it was late at night. She didn't care that she was the only person crazy enough to be out in weather like this—right now it matched her mood.

And as if to magnify her building temper, there was a flash of lightning above her, closely followed by a rumble of thunder.

Her anger built with every step she took.

She knew there was something between them. Any fool could see that.

How dared he call what had just happened a mistake?

He'd felt every single thing that she'd felt. He'd felt every tiny little spark and electric current that she had.

He'd been every bit as turned on as she'd been.

Did he think this was something she did every day—in the middle of the street?

No. She wouldn't let him treat her like that. Not for a second. Not in this lifetime.

Her footsteps quickened. Her normally bouncy curled hair was drenched, hanging in bedraggled rope-like swaths around her head. She reached up and rubbed her eye, coming away with a dark-washed smudge. What little mascara had been there was now obviously streaked down her face. But she didn't care.

She had no desire to go home and get changed. To strip off her wet clothes and climb under a warm duvet. The lightning flashed again. It was spurring her on, guiding her path straight to his door.

She climbed up his steps and put one finger on his doorbell, pressing hard and leaving it there. The other hand she clenched into a fist and banged on the door. She wouldn't be ignored. She wouldn't let Iain ignore whatever this was between them.

The door creaked open just as a rumble of thunder sounded overhead again and the dark clouds pitched above her.

Iain was bare-chested, obviously in the middle of stripping off his clothes. The dark circles under his eyes and shadow along his jaw only fed her fury even more.

'Lexi! What are you doing here?'

She pushed past him—not waiting to be asked to come in, and stood in the middle of his wide hallway, letting a huge puddle of rainwater form at her feet.

She clenched her jaw. 'You. Won't. Treat. Me. Like. That.' Every word was forced. Every word angrily controlled.

His hands were trembling as he closed the door behind her, shutting out the storm outside but not the one inside.

She said nothing. Stared him down. Watched the changing emotions on his face. She was strong enough for this. Whatever it might be.

She could see the pulse throbbing at the base of his neck, see every dark, curly chest hair standing on end.

But he didn't say a word. Not a single thing.

He just moved. And started kissing her like she'd never been kissed before.

CHAPTER SEVEN

IT WAS FIVE O'CLOCK in the morning and the first early streams of light were edging their way through the gap in the curtains. Lexi turned over in bed, her hand coming up automatically and touching her still-damp hair. It seemed impossible to believe that shaggy-haired Iain didn't possess a hairdryer, and her thick, long hair held the dampness, causing her to spend most of the night turning her pillow over.

'Wanna swap?' Iain was watching her with his dark brown eyes.

'Absolutely.' She smiled. 'I'm ruthless when it comes to bedding.' She grabbed the pillow he offered and sank down into the soft dryness, pushing the still-damp one in his direction.

He picked up a lock of her blonde hair. 'Doesn't matter if your hair is damp, Lexi. You still look beautiful.'

She shifted in the bed, instantly uncomfortable. 'You don't need to talk me into bed, Iain, I'm already here.'

His eyes widened. 'Why on earth would you think that?'

She pulled the light sheet a little closer to her body and sighed. 'I know I'm not beautiful, Iain. I've spent my life living in the shadow of the "world's most beautiful woman".' She lifted her fingers in the air to make imaginary quote marks. 'You just learn to accept that will never be you.'

Ian lifted his head and propped it up on his hand. 'What do you see when you look in the mirror, Lexi?'

She frowned. 'What do you mean?'

He shook his head. 'I'm betting you don't see what I do. Not even close.'

She pulled the sheet up above her breasts, as if shielding herself from him. She was almost too scared to ask the next question. 'What do you see?' she whispered.

He lifted a finger and traced it lightly down the side of her cheek. 'I see a gorgeous young woman, with beautiful skin, perfectly intact—not damaged by the sun in any way.' He ran his finger over her eyelids. 'I see the most beautiful blue eyes. There's a little hint of turquoise and they remind me of the sea next to a Caribbean island.' His finger dusted her eyelids. 'I see thick, dark lashes that most women would give their eye teeth for and a pair of lips that were exclusively designed for kissing me.'

She smiled and he leaned over and kissed her gently on the lips. She closed her eyes a little. 'Okay, so I'm starting to like that.'

His hand drifted under the sheet and she felt herself tense a little. He hadn't mentioned her surgery. Hadn't mentioned it at all. And it struck her as strange. He was a surgeon. He'd known from the very first time their bodies had made contact that she'd had surgery. And he had certainly appreciated her breasts last night.

The pads of his fingers caressed her shoulders then followed the curves of her body. He pulled the sheet back a little. 'I'd ask you who did them, but I might get a little jealous. Because they're perfect.' His finger danced along the almost invisible scar under one of her breasts.

'You really think so?' Her voice was hesitant. She'd expected him to criticise. For all he was a surgeon himself, he didn't seem to rate cosmetic surgery very highly.

He nodded slowly, his eyelids still heavy with fatigue. 'I just wonder why you felt as if you needed them.'

It was a natural question, particularly for a surgeon, but it instantly caused her to bristle.

For a second it crossed her mind to lie. To act with a whole lot of bravado. But she was done with pretending to be something she was not. She was Lexi Robbins and she was proud of who she was.

'I didn't want them. Not to begin with. My ex—Jack told me to get them. He wore me down, kept telling me my flat chest did nothing for him and it made me feel as if I wasn't worthy of our relationship.'

Anger flared instantly in Iain's eyes. 'What?' He sat up, his voice incredulous. 'Why on earth would he do that? You're gorgeous, Lexi—and

I'm sure you were absolutely perfect. What a complete—'

Her hand reached up and cut him off. 'Iain. Don't. I've spent a long time coming to terms with this. Jack never really loved me and it took a long time for me to understand that. Jack loved the *idea* of me. Who my parents were. The fact my name attracted attention. The fact my name meant we got invited to every fancy party in town.'

Iain's expletives filled the room. 'Of all the low-down, monkey-brained—'

'Stop that. Don't insult monkeys. They're highly intelligent creatures.'

But she could see the fire was still burning in his belly. 'I don't get it, Lexi. Why would you let anyone persuade you to have surgery? Didn't your surgeon ask you questions about why you were there? I thought he'd done a good job but now I'm not so sure.'

She shook her head. 'I gave him all the right answers, Iain. He didn't do anything wrong.' She sighed and lay back against the pillow again, her hands coming up and resting on her breasts.

'I've come to like my boobs. They've given me more confidence. They've made me feel better about myself. Deep down, I was never really happy with my shape—Jack just amplified my own feelings in a cruel way.'

There must have been something on her face, something about the way she said the words.

Iain's face darkened even further. 'Was that all he did?'

She hesitated as she felt a little flush of colour come to her cheeks. It seemed ridiculous. She'd just spent the night with Iain, was lying naked in bed with him, and she was embarrassed to say the words.

'What is it?' he coaxed, intertwining his fingers with hers.

'He said other things too. He didn't just comment on my breasts—or lack of them. He told me I should be taking lessons…for other things.'

It took a few seconds for the penny to drop and Lexi was cringing. It was bad enough that Jack had said those things in the first place. She'd never told another living soul about them.

Iain looked incredulous. 'He said what? How dared he?'

She looked down and shrugged her shoulders. 'I'm not the most experienced. I've only ever had a few long-term relationships.'

'And he thought he would criticise you?' Iain's voice was aghast. 'Lexi, he should have been grateful, honoured even that you let him get that close to you. That you trusted him enough to share yourself with him. He shouldn't have been criticising your technique!'

The fury of his words made her want to bury her head under the pillow. She kept her eyes averted. 'This isn't normal for me, Iain. This isn't what I do. I don't do—*this*.'

He put his finger under her chin and tilted her face up to look at his. 'I get that. And I didn't get that because I thought you were inexperienced.' He gave her little smile. 'I have no complaints at all—quite the contrary, in fact. I enjoyed every second. You were perfect.'

Was it wrong that those words gave her a little buzz all the way down to her toes? Was it wrong that she couldn't help but smile? Smile at the gorgeous, handsome, strapping man who was lying next to her in bed, telling her that he thought she was perfect?

Even though she hadn't realised she'd been holding it, her breath came out in a long, steady stream.

She looked back into his eyes. 'Everything has changed. I'm a different person than I used to be—and not just physically. I like how I look now. I'm comfortable in my own skin. I love the fact that I'm doing a job that makes me happy. I don't care that my parents don't appreciate it. I know the value of the job I do. I've raised more money in the last few weeks than even I thought possible. I've got another few trips overseas to speak to some more potential clients.' She ran her fingers along the stubble on his jaw. 'And I've got a whole host of plans for raising the pro-file of the Harley Street clinic, some of which include a hunky Scotsman...' she gave him a wink '...who might even wear a kilt for me.'

He rolled his eyes and she laughed, before roll-ing back onto her back and putting her hands on her breasts again. 'This is me, Lexi Robbins. Take me or leave me.'

Iain's hand came over and rested over one of hers. 'So you're happy?'

She nodded. 'Yes, Iain, I'm happy.'

His hand ran down the outside of the sheet, resting on her hip. She wondered if he was about to ask other questions about her abdominal scar. Would she answer truthfully? Did she feel as if she could?

He wrinkled his nose at her. 'Well, I'm not.'

Her stomach gave a little clench. What did he mean?

'I want to find Jack Parker and wring his neck with my bare hands until I squeeze every last breath out of him. I want to bang his head off a wall to try and knock some sense into him. I want to take a walk down a dark alley late at night and show him what I think about how he treated you.'

She was struck by the intensity of his words. Maybe it was the aftermath of their lovemaking that had provoked such deep emotions in him but she could tell from the sincerity in his brown eyes that he'd meant every word.

'Thank you,' she whispered. 'But this was about me dealing with things. I had to learn for myself that he wasn't what I thought. I had to value myself enough to not allow him to treat me that way. He was never physical, he never laid a hand on me. But his constant comments on my face and figure wore me down. I've never felt so free than when I flung him out of our flat and dumped his designer wardrobe out of the window. At that point, it was probably the best moment of my life.'

Iain lifted his hand and rested it between her breasts. 'But we both know that all beauty is superficial. I can make the most hideous person in the world look stunning on the outside. But it doesn't change what's in here. Who that person really is. There have never been truer words than "Beauty is only skin deep".'

There was genuine warmth in his words, a warmth that swept around her like a comfortable blanket, shielding her from everything else.

She could get used to this. She could get used to being shielded by Iain McKenzie.

'I want you to know, Lexi Robbins, that you are one of the most beautiful people I've ever met. Both inside and out. And no matter what happens in the future, where we both end up, I want you to keep that with you. And if any time you're feeling down, if you've had a bad day and can't face things, I want you to come back and remember *this* moment, here and now.'

In one way the words were a comfort, and in another they made her stomach clench again. She'd no idea what she expected from Iain— none of this had been planned. But there seemed to be a little edge to those words. As if he knew there would never be a future for them so he was just giving her this moment instead.

And the fact was she'd never felt so perfect as she did at this moment. She'd never felt so valued.

He stroked his fingers down her face again. 'We need to talk. There are some other things I need to tell you. But first I want to show you just how special you are.'

And for the next few hours he did.

* * *

By the time Iain woke up the sun was streaming through the windows. He turned to face Lexi. She was smiling. A real, genuine smile of contentment.

'How long have you been awake?'

She looked over at the clock. 'About ten minutes.' She lay back and stretched her arms above her head. 'I was waiting for you to make me breakfast,' she said with a glint in her eye.

'Do you have any preferences?'

'Do you have any food?'

He cringed. 'Have you already been up and looked through my cupboards?'

She touched his chin. 'You just strike me as a guy who doesn't do a weekly shop.'

He laughed. 'You're right. If you wanted dinner right now we'd be in trouble. But breakfast I can do. How does poached egg, toast and bacon sound?'

'Heavenly.' She glanced towards his en suite. 'Can I use your shower while you make breakfast?'

'Of course.' Iain pulled on his dressing-gown

and headed to the kitchen. His stomach was churning. He'd never brought a woman back to his London house before, let alone back to his bedroom. He'd spent so long partitioning these parts of his life and keeping himself away from people.

Of course he socialised when he had to. He kept in contact with some of his old friends in Edinburgh—but those were fleeting hello-good-bye moments. But since moving down to London he hadn't really been seeking the company of friends. He wasn't really looking for friends. He was only looking for partial distractions. And his gut told him Lexi Robbins could never fit into that category.

He started boiling water in one pan, put the bacon under the grill and the bread in the toaster. The coffee was easy, he had a bright and shiny machine he hardly used. All he had to do was flick a switch.

He turned, his eyes catching on a photo on the window ledge. A photo of Bonnie, sitting on top of a hill in Edinburgh on a sunny day. She had wrapped her long pink flowered dress around her legs to stop it flapping in the wind and her hair was completely windswept.

Something curled inside him. It was going to be the three of them sitting in this kitchen, having breakfast. He wasn't sure how he felt about that. He wasn't sure if he was ready for that.

Everything with Lexi was so new. Attraction aside, he didn't even know how he felt about her yet. Sure, she was beautiful. Sure, she was intelligent. But did that add up to anything else?

For a split second he considered putting the photo in a drawer. But as quickly as the thought flew into his head he pushed it aside. He could never treat Bonnie as if she hadn't existed. He owed her so much more than that.

And Lexi was no fool. She knew nothing about his past. She would ask about the photo on the window ledge. It was if a dozen little pinpricks started on his shoulders at once. He would tell her. He would tell her about Bonnie. She'd been a big part of his life and she deserved her place there.

The bacon sizzled just as the coffee machine started to splutter and the water in the pot boiled. He dropped in the eggs and pulled out some plates and cutlery.

Lexi appeared a few minutes later, looking like the kind of pin-up poster a teenage boy would have on his bedroom wall.

She'd clipped her hair haphazardly on top of her head and pulled one of his long-sleeved blue shirts from his cupboard. The bottom buttons were fastened and the top two left tantalisingly open. Along with her long legs and pink toe-nails, the effect was stunning.

She shrugged. 'I don't think my dress will ever recover. It's spent the night on the floor in a sodden mess. Hope you don't mind.'

'Of course I don't.' He set the coffee on the table. 'Cappuccino okay for you?'

'Of course.' She lifted the coffee cup to her lips and smiled. 'Don't be too good at this. I might get comfortable.'

There was that little tumble in his stomach again. He didn't know how to react to that. The toast popped and he buttered it and placed it on the table, alongside the bacon and the newly poached eggs.

Lexi started piling food on her plate and Iain watched with pleasure. It was the second time he'd eaten with Lexi, and for all her slim frame she wasn't afraid to eat. Thank goodness. He couldn't stand being around a picky eater.

Iain took a few mouthfuls then set his fork down. He didn't even get a chance to say a word.

'You said you wanted to talk, Iain. What is it? Is this where you tell me this is a wham-bam, thank you, ma'am?'

Boy, she was direct. Another thing he liked about her. This was getting harder all the time.

He shook his head and took a quick drink of his thick, strong coffee. He took a deep breath, but when he exhaled it came out more like a sigh.

'Spit it out, Scots boy.'

He nodded and pointed to the window ledge before he changed his mind. 'I wanted to introduce you to someone.'

Lexi looked up at the photo of the pretty dark-haired woman. 'She's lovely. Who is she? Your sister?'

'My wife.'

Lexi set her cup on the table, her face frozen. 'Please tell me you're not still married. I don't sleep with married men.' She was deadly serious and her face was deathly pale.

'I'm widowed,' he said quickly.

There was a visible sigh of relief from across the table. She took a deep breath, her eyes full of sympathy for him. He wasn't sure that was what he wanted. He'd had enough darned sympathy to last a lifetime. He just wanted her to understand.

'I'm really sorry about your loss, Iain. I can't imagine what that feels like.'

There was a tight feeling in his chest. A kettle-bell from the gym had just positioned itself on his chest, pushing the air out of his lungs and making him struggle for breath. He was going to see this through. He was. Once he'd told her, that was it—it was out there.

'It won't surprise you to know I don't talk

about my personal life much. That's why I came down to London. To get away from things. The only person who knows what happened is Leo.'

'Don't worry. I won't breathe a word.'

He tried to find the words in his head. He wasn't just doing this for himself, he was doing it for her too. 'Bonnie—my wife—died giving birth to our twins. There were complications. My son and daughter died too.'

Her hand had gone automatically to her mouth and her eyes had widened in shock. This wasn't your everyday conversation.

He put his elbows on the table for a second and put his head in his hands. He was trying not to let the familiar wave of emotions wash over him. He needed to keep himself together.

He ran his tongue along his dry lips. 'I wanted you to know that when I walked away last night—I wasn't walking away from you. It wasn't about you.' He pressed his hand to his chest. 'It was about me feeling guilty. I haven't been with anyone since my wife died.'

'Oh, Iain…' There were tears glistening in her

eyes and in a second she was up on her bare feet, walking round the kitchen table and standing behind him, linking her hands around his neck and resting her head on his shoulder.

They stayed like that for a few minutes. He could feel the rise and fall of her chest behind him, feel her warm breath on his cheek. He lifted up his hand and linked it with hers.

'Lexi, I just want you to know—'

'Don't say it.'

He pulled her hand, adjusting his position in the chair until he was sitting sideways and could pull her onto his lap.

'I don't know about anything. I can't promise you anything. Because I don't know if I'm ready. I don't know if I'm there yet.' She looked so young, so vulnerable. The very last thing he wanted to do was hurt her.

He put his finger under her chin and pulled her head up to meet his eyes. They were almost nose to nose and he had the clearest view he'd ever had of her beautiful blue eyes. 'I want you to know that I think you're gorgeous. I think you're very desirable. And if I make a mess of things here, it's because there's something wrong with *me*, not you. You're every man's dream come true.' He lowered his voice. 'But not every man deserves you, Lexi. And not every man is ready for you.'

There was a waver in her eyes, a sign of hesitation. Then she took a deep breath, her chest rose and her shoulders straightened. Her fingers wound their way through his shaggy brown hair. 'Thank you for telling me about your wife, Iain. I appreciate this is hard. And it's new. I won't tell anyone about your wife. And I guess we can just wait to see how things go.'

She smiled at him, and it was an older, more resigned smile. 'I'm not looking for you to save me. After my last experience I'm just looking for someone to treat me with respect and value my opinions. How about we go from there?'

He could see she was holding back. He could see there was something in her eyes that she was keeping from him. Guarding herself and guarding her heart. The sensible option. And he respected that. He could live with that, because he hadn't told her everything yet. That might come later.

She stood up. 'You're still going to be grumpy at the clinic, though, aren't you?'

He took a bite of his toast. 'Obviously. Why change the habit of a lifetime?' He looked at the clock. 'Are you due there today?'

She nodded and looked down at the pale blue shirt. 'I don't have any appointments until later today—and then some into the evening. I have a few interviews lined up with some national papers and I still need to edit your interview. Oh, and get you to pose for some publicity shots.'

'I am *not* wearing a kilt.'

She tilted her head to the side and folded her arms. 'I might be able to think of a way to persuade you. How much time have you got?'

'A few hours. I need to go to the Lighthouse to check on one of my patients. But they aren't expecting me until around eleven.' He abandoned the toast. He much preferred the other offer. 'How do you think you can persuade me?'

'Have you got a bath? A big bath?' She had

that gleam in her eye as she took his hand and led him towards the stairs.

Her voice drifted along the corridor. 'And what I'd really like is some bubbles...'

CHAPTER EIGHT

IAIN GLANCED AT the clock on the wall. 'Lexi, are you ready?' He didn't want to be late.

She appeared instantly at his side. He tried not to let his eyes automatically run up and down the length of her body—but, boy, was it hard. Her perfume was already assaulting his senses and rejigging his memory from the night before.

It was making his skin prickle and resurrecting a whole host of feelings of guilt. He tried to push them away. She was dressed conservatively. A plain cream blouse, knee-length navy skirt and flats. But she still managed to carry it off with panache. The sooner he finished with this the better. He hated the fact he didn't think he could control his body's responses around her. The last thing he needed was other people suspecting something was going on.

This was the last part of the filming—a review

of a little Chinese boy he'd performed surgery on a few days ago. He stopped just outside the door and nodded to the cameraman, who started filming.

'Okay, today we're going to look in on An. He's a six-year-old Chinese boy with a facial deformity—hemifacial microsomia. It's a condition that affects the bone, muscle, fat and nerves of the lower part of the face. The deformities are on a spectrum. They can range from a mild presentation with slight asymmetry to severe absence of facial structures. It's a progressive disorder and becomes more apparent as the child grows.'

'How common is it?' asked Lexi.

'It's the second most common facial deformity and affects around one in five thousand six hundred births. It's equally common in males and females.'

Lexi halted at the door and he wondered about her reaction. Please don't let her grimace when she sees the child. An's asymmetrical features were apparent, even at a young age. He had many more years of surgery ahead of him.

He tapped her shoulder as they walked in and kept talking to the camera. 'One side of An's face is growing normally. The other isn't. The surgery I did a few days ago was a mandibular correction to allow for normal maxillary growth. It means An's dental structures and jaw will be in better alignment.'

He was still watching Lexi from the corner of his eye. She had her head tilted to one side and looked as if she was concentrating fiercely. She was watching An and his mother talk in hushed voices. He glanced towards the doorway again, waiting for the translator. Speaking Chinese was not in his repertoire.

But it appeared to be in Lexi's.

She walked over and knelt next to the little boy and his mother, trying a few hesitant words. The woman's eyebrows shot skywards and after a few seconds she replied haltingly.

Lexi smiled and tried again. This time she was a little more relaxed and the words flowed more freely. The exchange lasted a few minutes. Iain couldn't believe his eyes. How did she know Chinese?

He took a few steps closer. 'Lexi?'

She looked up. 'I thought I recognised the language. It's Gan with a Nanchang dialect.'

'How on earth do you know that?'

A wrinkle appeared across her brow. It was obvious she was choosing her words carefully. 'Do you remember I told you I spent the summer with my aunt?'

He nodded.

'My aunt did lots of charity work. At that time most of her work was in some of the Chinese orphanages. She took me over there for a whole summer. It was the best summer of my life.'

'You learned a Chinese dialect in one summer?'

'I still go back,' she said quietly. 'Away from the spotlight. Every few years Jo and I go back to that same orphanage. I feel a real connection with it. I've spent a long time learning the language, the particular dialect. It makes the work so much more rewarding when I can converse with the children.

'Some of those children were taken away from their parents against their will. The parents couldn't afford to pay the fine for having more than one child. It's awful. But we've tried to make things better. We have links with social services around the world and some of the children get adopted internationally.'

'So, An is from the same area?'

She nodded. 'Yes. I'm not completely fluent, but I can easily make myself understood. You don't need to wait for an interpreter.'

Iain hesitated for a second. He was trying not to let his mouth hang open. But Lexi had just rendered him speechless.

This was not what he had expected. And he was almost ashamed to think that.

He'd been up close and personal with her. He knew she was much deeper than people assumed. But it was obvious he'd only scratched the surface—only got to know a little about the woman underneath the pretty façade.

From her teenage years Lexi had spent summer after summer helping out at a Chinese orphanage. This was more than charity work for her. She was committed to this. Committed enough to learn the language.

He'd spent a summer at a Romanian orphanage himself, operating on children with cleft lips and palates. He knew how much it sucked you in. How you would do anything to help. How you could think about nothing else.

This was a whole new part of Lexi Robbins he hadn't counted on.

'Iain? Are we doing this?'

He nodded, embarrassed by his long silence. 'Of course…thank you.'

He knelt down next to An, who was perched on his mother's knee. The stitches on the skin along the little boy's jaw had healed well. 'Ask him how he's managing to eat.'

Lexi nodded and spoke quietly to his mother, listening to her reply and letting An answer too. She turned to Iain. 'He's fed up with soft foods.' She gave him a smile. 'He wants some chips.'

Iain smiled. 'Can you ask him to open his mouth so I can have a look at his dentition? Some of his teeth have been affected by the re-positioning of his jaw.'

Lexi only took a second to ask the question and An opened his mouth a little hesitantly.

Iain bent down and looked inside, using a small torch, 'Everything looks as though it's healing well. I see no reason he can't have a more substantial diet.'

Lexi translated quickly. An's face was still bruised and slightly swollen and his attempt at a smile lopsided. But it was the most satisfying thing that Iain could see.

'Can you ask him about pain relief? If he's going to eat a bit more he might need his analgesics adjusted for the next few days.'

Lexi took a few minutes, taking her time while she spoke to An and his mother. She made it seem like the most natural thing in the world. It was obvious she wasn't completely fluent, but she had more than a grasp of the language, and An and his mother seemed to appreciate being able to communicate with a member of staff.

Lexi turned around from where she was kneeling on the floor and touched Iain's leg. The warmth of her hand startled him, as did her position. He moved quickly out of her reach, before her touch could have any affect. 'An hasn't been talking too much as he finds the jaw movements painful. He probably does need his analgesics adjusted.'

Iain nodded. 'Let them know I'll take care of that now.' He lifted the chart and walked over the nurses' station to talk to the nurse allocated to An. Lexi stayed where she was, continuing to talk to An and his mother.

They loved her already. It was obvious. She was writing a few things on a piece of paper along with a little picture and telling them what they meant. It was obvious there had been a few key things they had wanted to communicate to the staff and hadn't been able to. Lexi was doing her best to facilitate that. She was doing her very best for an unknown mother and child she'd just met.

It made his stomach twist. Lexi's nature was sweet and kind. This shouldn't be unexpected for him. But seeing it, right before his eyes, was just a little different.

He was used to Lexi Robbins, Head of PR. He'd also experienced Lexi Robbins, sultry, sexy woman.

But Lexi Robbins, humanitarian, was a whole

different ball game. Now he understood where the passion in her eyes came from when she spoke about the charity work. It wasn't just all part of her PR game. It was how she really *felt*.

And that made him uncomfortable.

It made him feel too close.

She was unsettling him, in more ways than one. She was much more than a pretty face.

But the thing that worried him most was just how much more he wanted to know.

The knock on the door work her up. Eek! She'd overslept.

She dashed to the door, trying to shove her arms into her dressing-gown. She pulled the door open. 'Iain. I'm sorry. Give me five minutes and I promise you I'll be ready.' She didn't wait for an answer, just dashed to the bedroom to throw on some jeans and a jumper.

A few minutes later she found him in her kitchen, stirring a cup of black of coffee. 'Inside or out?'

'What?' He looked confused.

'You haven't told me where we're going. What kind of jacket do I need?'

He smiled. 'Dress up warm.'

She raised her eyebrows and ducked back into her bedroom, pulling out a pair of red leather gloves and a red woolly hat with a huge pom-pom on top and big flaps to cover her ears. She stuffed it on top of her blonde hair and pulled on a thick black jacket and fleecy black boots.

It was freezing in London. Not wet or drizzly. It was completely dry, just very, very cold.

'I'm ready.' She marched into the kitchen and took a quick drink of the coffee Iain had made for her. It wasn't a skinny caramel latte, but he'd made it perfectly. Maybe this was all just a little too good to be true.

Iain held the door open for her. 'Then let's go. Time to have some fun.'

They rode on the Tube and got off at Tower Hill. They walked out of the Tube station and round the corner to face the impressive façade of the Tower of London.

'We're going sightseeing?'

He nodded. 'I haven't been yet. I've been in

London two years and I've hardly seen a thing.' He walked up to the ticket booth. 'Do we want to see the Crown Jewels too?'

She didn't hesitate for a second. 'Absolutely. It's my favourite part.'

He took their tickets and reached out to take her hand as they walked towards the main entrance, where impressive Beefeaters in their black and red outfits stood.

Iain stopped for a few seconds. 'Wow. It's some place. Have you been here much?'

She nodded. 'Not as much as you think. Last time was around eight years ago.' She stopped and looked back at the impressive White Tower. 'Why did you pick here?'

He looked a little sheepish. 'I actually wanted to go to Buckingham Palace but I didn't realise it's only open in the summer for tours.'

'It's fabulous.' Something tickled in her stomach. July would be the time for the tours to start at Buckingham Palace. That was five months away. 'Maybe we can go some other time.'

'Maybe.' It sounded so noncommittal and she

tried not to feel disappointed. Iain had already told her he didn't know where this would go.

She pulled him further along where she could see a small crowd gathering. 'Let's listen to one of the Yeoman tours. They know everything about the Tower's history, it's great fun.'

They joined the crowd and waited for a few minutes for the tour to start. Lexi was right. It was fascinating. He'd never realised just how treacherous a place the Tower of London had been. He watched as the Yeoman showed them where the boats used to moor with their prisoners and royal victims at Traitor's Gate. He showed them the place where the two young princes were supposedly imprisoned and perhaps killed.

Lexi leaned her head against his shoulder as they listened to the tour. There was a young woman next to her, trying to juggle three kids—a baby in a pouch next to her breasts, a toddler strapped into a buggy and a four-year-old who was looking distinctly bored and kept wandering off. The woman looked tired and was struggling to hear what the Yeoman was saying. Lexi touched her arm and gave her a smile. 'If it's okay with you, how about I entertain your oldest for a little while?'

The woman nodded and gave her a grateful smile. They were standing on Tower Green. Lexi could walk about freely and still be safely in the mother's sight.

She walked over and bent down next to the dark-headed little girl. Her heart gave a squeeze. The little girl was gorgeous. Her hair was in bunches and wearing a purple coat. 'Hi, there. I'm Lexi. How about I tell you some stories about this place?'

The little girl scowled at her. Lexi pointed over at her mother. 'Your mum says it's okay.' She gave her mother a wave. 'What's your name.'

'Lucy.'

Lexi held out her hand. 'Good. I'm Lexi. Pleased to meet you.'

Lucy gave a sigh. 'My feet are sore and Damian is in the buggy.' She rolled her eyes.

Lexi held out her hands. 'Fancy a carry?'

Lucy's eyes brightened and she let her herself be lifted into Lexi's arms. As the tour moved along little by little, Lexi stayed only a few feet away from the mother, whispering in Lucy's ear and pointing out various things along the way.

Iain watched carefully. Lexi seemed so at ease. She was obviously used to children. She'd already told Iain about her work at the Chinese orphanage and everything she did showed him her natural affinity for children.

A heavy feeling started to descend over him. Lexi was his first step back to a normal life. He'd promised her nothing.

She spun Lucy backwards in her arms, letting her lean back and throw her arms out, imitating the ravens around about them. Their hair flew outwards as they spun, the smiles on their faces completely and utterly spontaneous. Lexi was a natural.

And he didn't like it.

It was a horrible admission. But Iain hadn't planned on thinking such thoughts on what he'd wanted to be a nice day out.

But watching Lexi was making him ache. He was wasting his time with her. Here was a woman who had the word 'mother' stamped all over her. What would she think when she found out what he'd done? If she'd any sense at all she would run in the other direction.

What woman would want to be with a man who'd persuaded his wife to take the final chance of IVF that had led to her death?

He looked around Tower Green. Families everywhere. Families happy and smiling. And he knew. He knew he could never set foot in a delivery room again. Not after his last experience.

And Lexi would want a family of her own. How could he explain? She was kneeling on the ground with Lucy right now, telling her some long and obviously gory tale by the actions she was doing. Right on cue, Lucy's mouth formed a wide O. She slapped her hand across her mouth as Lexi let out a peal of laughter.

Right before his eyes was the reason he should stop all this. He could never be the man that she needed.

But Lexi turned and pushed her hat further back on her head. Her blonde hair was sticking out all round and she shot him the most dazzling smile. The Yeoman was reaching the end of the walking tour at the Medieval Tower.

She mouthed over to him, 'Crown jewels?'

He nodded. She'd already told him it was her favourite part. They joined the queue with Lucy's mother behind them. She was looking calmer, more relaxed. She leaned over and whispered to the two of them, 'It's dark in here, isn't it? The two little ones will fall asleep as soon as we get inside.'

They queued quietly as Lexi started to whisper stories of secret princesses to Lucy. The inside of the display was dark, surrounded by armed guards, who were happy to talk to the visitors about some of the jewels on display.

Lucy's little face gaped at the huge glittering Cullianan diamond in the sovereign's sceptre.

'I don't think there is a magical fairy kingdom inside the stone,' Iain whispered.

'Shh!' Lexi put her finger to her lips, 'Spoilsport,' she whispered.

They oohed over the Imperial state crown and Lucy was highly disappointed she couldn't try it on. 'But I'm a princess too,' she said huffily.

'I know you are,' said Lexi, 'and I'm sure when we get to the gift shop I'll be able to buy you a crown of your own.'

And sure enough she did. It was early afternoon by the time they'd finished at the Tower. 'I'm sorry our afternoon got hijacked,' she said to Iain as they made their way to the exit.

'No, you're not,' he said, shaking his head. 'You looked like you were having the time of your life. What stories were you telling her?'

Lexi smiled. 'Stories about the evil ravens stealing fairies and the fairies fighting back by hiding in the crown jewels.'

'All totally based on reality, then?'

She nodded solemnly. 'Based on a four-year-old girl's reality.' She tapped the side of her nose. 'That's the trick to keeping them quiet.'

'Well, you certainly managed to master that.'

She smiled up at him as he reached for her hand and gave it a little squeeze. 'Let's go for a walk down to Tower Bridge,' she said.

Even though it was still cold, the day was bright and sunny. The path down next to the bridge was busy, filled with street acts and various parties on tours. They bought coffee from a street vendor and sat on a bench, people-watching.

Lexi seemed relaxed and happy next to him. If they looked along the river a little they could see Kate's. 'Are you going there today?'

Iain nodded. 'I'll go in later. I have a few patients to check over. It won't take long.'

She ran her tongue along her lips. Her hat was sitting in her lap now and her blonde hair was blowing in the breeze. She didn't seem to mind at all that it was all over the place. In fact, for the daughter of a supermodel, Lexi didn't seem to care at all about her appearance. She hadn't looked in a mirror once since they'd met today.

She was gorgeous, of course. But it helped him realise how far down the list she put superficial things. Another plus point for Lexi.

If only that didn't make him squirm. Because every good point about Lexi made him realise how they couldn't really be a match. There must be a whole host of guys out there who would want to snatch her up. To admire her beauty, good spirit and work ethic. A hundred guys out there who want to settle down with her and have a family.

She leaned over and gave him a gentle kiss on the lips. There was a kind of glazed look behind her smile. She was squinting at him in the sunshine as she reached up and ran her fingers through his hair.

'It's not exactly the usual look, is it?' she said, tugging at his shaggy hair.

'What do you mean?' He was distracted by her lips and blue eyes and only looked up when she gave his hair an extra tug.

'Most surgeons go for the ultra-short look.'

'I'm not most surgeons,' he growled.

'I get that.'

'Just imagine me shipwrecked on a mysterious island. This is the natural look for me.'

'Good, because I like it. It suits you.' She gave him a cheeky wink. 'Now, don't ever cut it. I might go off you.' She stood up. 'So, fancy a late dinner at mine?'

She said the words so easily. Probably never expecting him to hesitate. But he did. This was his chance. This was his opportunity to let her spread her wings and fly. To stop any chance of him hurting her. But there was still a little something in her eyes. Still a little lack of confidence.

So he smiled, standing up and taking her hand. 'I think I can manage that.' He changed his mind, dropping her hand and wrapping his arm around her shoulder. She was closer this way.

Eventually he would have to let her go.

Eventually he would have to tell her the truth.

Just not right now.

CHAPTER NINE

'LEXI, CAN I speak to you a minute, please?'

Ethan Hunter was leaning on her doorframe. *He's still not using his stick.* It was her first thought and she quickly pushed it out of her head. It was none of her business.

She pushed her chair back and stood up, walking over towards the door. 'No problem, Ethan. What can I do for you?'

She was very busy, and between an influx of high-profile clients, thanks to her PR campaign, her nights with Iain and her charity work, she hardly had a moment to think. But Ethan very rarely bothered her and she wanted to give him the attention he deserved.

Ethan looked a little uncomfortable. Was that his leg again, or was he just choosing his words carefully?

'Lexi, I wanted to ask you about something.

I've seen some paperwork lying about and heard some of the other surgeons talking about Fair Go. Can you tell me what it is?'

Lexi straightened her shoulders and put on her brightest smile. 'Why don't you come and sit down, Ethan? I'm happy to fill you in on all the details of Fair Go. Can I get you some tea or coffee?'

Ethan shook his head and sat down in the leather high-backed armchair opposite her desk. He probably didn't even realise the visible sweep of relief that came across his face as he took the weight off his leg.

Lexi shuffled some papers on her desk until she found what she was looking for. 'Here it is. Fair Go—it's a great name, isn't it? Named after Olivia Fairchild, the nurse who started it.'

She looked up in time to see Ethan visibly pale. Maybe his leg gave him more pain than he let on?

She moved on. 'It's an African-based charity focusing on helping adults and children affected by war. It's a small charity right now, but with our backing Olivia is hoping she will be able to assist more victims. She has several cases already that could do with transport to the UK for specialist surgery.' She smiled over at Ethan. 'I take it you'll be keen to take part?'

It seemed an obvious question. She knew that Ethan had been a victim of war himself so it seemed only natural he would want to help others. It just seemed odd his brother hadn't mentioned it—but, then again, she couldn't really fathom the relationship between the brothers. And she knew better than to interfere in other families' problems.

Ethan's voice was strained. 'Of course I'll take part. I knew another charity was being proposed for the clinic—I just hadn't heard the details yet. That's why I asked Iain if he'd be willing to participate too. I take it he was happy to help?'

Lexi felt an odd rush of colour to her cheeks. Oh, no. Just the mention of Iain's name was causing her to blush. Talk about giving herself away.

'Yes, yes. Well, you know Iain. I had to persuade him a little.' Had she really managed to say that without turning beetroot red?

'I'm sorry I haven't done your interview yet,

Lexi.' Ethan had the good grace to look a little shame-faced. 'It's just not really my thing. I prefer to stay out of the spotlight. I am happy to support the charity work, though.'

He was staring at the paper on her desk—the one with the details of Olivia Fairchild's charity. And he was looking at it with such ferocity that she knew something else was going on entirely. She wouldn't like to be in Leo Hunter's shoes right now.

She decided to give him an out. 'I spent three weeks chasing you for an interview, Ethan—I can take a hint. Iain gave in after two. I think we'll be able to use his interview for some very effective publicity. I finished the edits on it last night and we're ready to release it online in a few days. So I think I can release you from your obligation.'

She saw a little tension sag out of his shoulders and he stood up from the chair. 'Lexi, just to let you know. We had news yesterday of some other big-name clients. Sheikh Abdullah's wife, Lydia Jones the newscaster and Violet Ingram the equestrian who fell in the recent Games, to name a few. They're all coming here for surgery. I don't know what you've been doing out there—but it's obviously working.'

His dark hazel eyes were full of sincerity. 'Thanks, Lexi. This will make a world of difference for us, particularly around our charity work.'

'That's why you pay me, Ethan. I'm just happy you think I'm doing a good job.' She watched as he walked to the door, his limp still visible.

This was the longest conversation she'd ever had with Ethan Hunter. She didn't know if he'd always been this quiet or if it was since his return from his tour of duty in Afghanistan. It was obvious he'd been injured in the field. But she wasn't entirely sure what those injuries were. Just that while it was obvious he wasn't back to full fitness yet, it was equally obvious that he wasn't really ready to accept that.

She just hoped she hadn't stoked some still-smouldering fire between the brothers by telling Ethan about the Fair Go charity.

It seemed ridiculous. A number of other members of the clinic knew about Fair Go. Any one of them could have told Ethan about it.

So why was she hoping against hope that he wouldn't tell Leo it had been her?

'Time for coffee?'

The voice at the door startled her and she smiled as Carrie, one of the receptionists, appeared. Truth was, she didn't really have time to breathe let alone have coffee but she needed a break. And she needed some fresh air. She nodded. 'How about the coffee house at the end of the street? I could do with a walk.'

Carrie nodded and waved the purse she was holding in her hand. 'I was hoping you might say that. Let's go.'

They walked down the street swiftly. Lexi never did anything slowly and she was trying her best not to glance at her watch.

'So where have you been? I've hardly seen you these last few weeks.'

'I know. I've been rushed off my feet with the publicity campaign for the clinic and the charities.' She counted off on her fingers. 'In the last fourteen days I've been to Spain, Switzerland, Dubai and Belgium. I'm frazzled. And I'm due to launch the video interview of Iain in the next few days.'

Carrie nodded. She was smiling but Lexi could tell she wasn't really taking in everything she said.

She pushed open the door to the coffee house at the end of the street and grabbed the only free table. Neither of them needed to look at the menu. Lexi smiled at the waitress. 'Usual coffee—skinny latte with sugar-free caramel and...' she smiled over at the cake counter '...I'll have the raspberry and cream sponge, please.'

'And I'll have a cappuccino and a piece of the carrot cake, please.'

Lexi smiled as Carrie adjusted herself in the chair. 'Ooh, you're eating today. You never normally eat mid-morning.'

Carrie fumbled in her bag and pulled a white envelope out and pushed it across the table with a nervous smile.

Lexi felt her stomach flip over. *Keep smiling,* she told herself. She already knew what would be in the envelope. This had happened to her too many times already.

She went onto automatic pilot. She pulled the scan image from the envelope and let out a little gasp of surprise, trying the whole time not to think about how this moment would never be hers. She placed the black and white print out down, easily seeing the shape of the little baby with its curved spine, larger than average head and little limbs pointing upwards. She leaned over the table. 'Congratulations, Carrie, I'm delighted for you. When is your due date?'

Carrie's face flushed with pleasure. 'Tenth of September. I had my scan last week when I was twelve weeks.'

'And are you keeping okay?'

Carrie shrugged. 'I can't eat first thing in the morning because I feel really lousy. But by now—mid-morning—I'm ravenous.'

'So that's why the change in eating habits.'

The waitress appeared and put the coffees and cakes on the table, and Carrie didn't waste any time in digging in.

Lexi pressed her lips together. She was happy

for her friend. She really was. And she'd been through this a dozen times before. She'd resigned herself years before to the fact she wouldn't have kids naturally. She kept close ties with the orphanages—adoption would be her way to a future family. And she was looking forward to it—when the time was right.

But something had happened in the last two weeks, since she'd sat in that kitchen with Iain and looked into his eyes as he'd told her about losing his wife and twins. Her heart had broken for him. It truly had.

But something else had happened.

Her confidence and inner strength now had a tiny chip in the armour.

Iain and his wife had obviously wanted to have a family. Which meant that Iain had wanted a family of his own. Logic told her that even though his wife was gone, eventually his brain would go down that path again. That path of wanting to share his life with a woman who could have his children.

A path it wasn't possible for her to go down.

Carrie was guzzling her cake and coffee. And

she did look different. Lexi wondered why she hadn't noticed. Carrie had a little glow about her, her hair was thick and glossy and there was added sparkle in her eyes.

Carrie looked up. 'I wanted to tell you first before I tell anyone else. I know they will be fine about maternity leave and everything, but I just wanted to talk to you first.'

Lexi reached across the table and squeezed her hand. 'Thank you. I'm delighted for you—really I am.' Even though there were a million tiny butterflies taking flight in her stomach. The raspberry and cream sponge was beautiful but she could barely touch it.

She hated herself right now. She'd never felt more than a fleeting pang before when a friend had told her they were pregnant.

But what she hated more than anything right now was the remote possibility that because of her budding relationship with Iain, she might be feeling a tiny bit jealous.

Jealous. What a horrible word.

'What's going on with Iain McKenzie?'

'What?' She dropped the fork she'd been holding for the last few minutes.

Carrie was smiling. 'Our grumpy Scotsman isn't quite so grumpy. We're all wondering what's happened. Do you know anything?'

'Me? No.' The words came out too quickly, falling over themselves in their haste.

Carrie put her fork down. 'Lexi?' Her eyebrows were raised.

Oh, no. Carrie had that look on her face. That you'd-better-tell-me-everything-right-now look.

Lexi started shaking her head and focusing intently on the raspberry sponge, which all of a sudden she could eat easily. 'I've no idea what's going on with Iain. I've just told you I've not been around. I've been flying everywhere and barely had a minute to myself.' She popped a big piece of sponge into her mouth to stop herself saying anything else.

'Whatever you say, Lexi. But it's a remarkable coincidence that Iain appeared to get a whole lot brighter after your interview.' She lifted her hand and gave Lexi a wink. 'But if you say you know nothing, that's fine with me.'

The waitress came over and placed the bill on the table and Carrie had it in a flash. She waved it at Lexi. 'But it'll cost you!'

Lexi grabbed the bill and swallowed the big lump of cake in her throat. Everything was still so new with Iain. She didn't want to tell Carrie that in between flights to here, there and everywhere she'd either been sleeping at Iain's or he'd been sleeping at her place.

And if carrot cake was the price of Carrie's silence, that was good enough for her.

Lexi knocked on the door of Leo's office. She was trying to put all thoughts of the last time she'd been in here out of her mind. The thought of ending up with Iain lying on top of her made her blush. She only hoped the colour she felt flooding her cheeks would not be obvious to Leo.

'Come in,' came the deep voice behind the door.

She opened it. Leo was sitting behind his desk with the phone cradled between his shoulder and face, while he scribbled furiously in front of him. He gestured to Lexi to come in and sit down in front of his desk.

She gave him a wide smile and settled into the comfortable chair. Leo had a smile on his face, and it was so nice to see.

There had been so many changes in him over the last few weeks—all to do with his engagement to Lizzie Birch, the head nurse at the Hunter Clinic. Leo had always been good at his job but his personal life and his relationship with his brother had always seemed rocky. It was so nice to see him with a genuine, permanent smile on his face.

He put down the phone. 'Sorry about that, Lexi.' He shuffled some papers on his desk until he found what he was looking for. A printout of the accounts and charitable donations that Lexi had sent him. He stood up. 'That's quite a pile you've sent me.' He looked around his desk. There was barely any of rich wood surface visible. 'What do you say we go through to the conference room and spread these out?' He smiled. 'Lizzie left us some doughnuts for the meeting.'

Lexi stood back up. 'Perfect. You get the doughnuts, I'll get the coffee.'

She walked through to the conference room and left her papers on the desk, then crossed the corridor to the kitchen and loaded the pods into the machine. Perfect cappuccinos in two minutes flat.

She could hear voices as she approached the conference room. Its doors were wide open. Her steps slowed as she recognised Ethan's voice.

She hesitated. She was reluctant to go and interrupt them, even though she was supposed to be having a meeting with Leo right now. Tension seemed to emanate from both of them as soon as they were in the same room.

Leo sounded happier today. She could hear his deep voice easily. 'I wanted to let you know that Lizzie and I have set a date.'

'What? That's great. Congratulations, Leo. When is it?' Lexi felt relieved. Ethan did sound happy for his brother. Maybe things had eased between them?

'It's the last Saturday in April at Claridge's.'

'Wow. You don't hang about. Something else you want to tell me, brother?'

'What? No. Not yet, anyway.' There was a little edge to his tone. As if there was a smile on his face as he was saying the words.

'And are we going to have to remortgage the clinic to pay for it?'

Leo let out a laugh. 'No, that's all under control.' His voice went a little quieter. 'It was Lizzie's dream to get married there and I plan on giving her exactly what she wants.'

There was a little pause then Ethan replied, 'Making Lizzie happy is exactly what you should do.'

The edge of the cups had heated up and Lexi shifted her fingers to try and avoid being burnt. Maybe it was safe to go in now? She stepped closer to the door.

'So—I wanted to ask you a question.' Her foot stopped mid-air. Maybe not.

'What is it?'

She was close enough now to see both men. Ethan was leaning heavily on the table—still not using the walking stick that he should. Leo was sitting opposite him, his hand pulling at the edge of his ear. The way he did when he was uncomfortable.

'I wanted to ask you to be my best man.' The words came out in a rush.

There was a pause. A heavy silence in the air.

Just say yes, Lexi willed Ethan. She shifted her fingers on the cups again. *Say yes before I burn myself.*

'I don't think so, Leo.' Ethan's voice was low, so low Lexi couldn't believe he'd just said those words. She must have misheard.

'Why not?' She cringed. She could hear the tension in Leo's voice, no matter how he tried to hide it.

'I just don't think it's a good idea. Ask Declan or Edward—you've known them for a long time. They'd do a better job than me.'

Lexi could almost hear the long intake of breath from Leo. She could only imagine how hurt he felt right now. Even if he wasn't showing it.

From this angle she could see him paste a

smile on his face. 'You never were very good at speeches, were you, Ethan?'

'Rubbish. Whether you wrote them for me or not.'

It was an easy let-off. Even though he was obviously hurt, Leo had decided not to enter into a spat with his brother. His voice went a little lower. 'I just thought I should ask you first. You were the one to tell me to get my act together and sort out things with Lizzie.'

'That's because I'm the smart one in this family—and don't you forget it.'

Ethan had turned and headed towards the door. The conversation was clearly over.

'Sorry, Lexi, didn't see you there.'

She pasted a fake smile on her face. 'You'd better not have eaten my doughnut, Ethan Hunter. You could be in big trouble.'

He winked. 'Why break the habit of a lifetime?'

Lexi walked into the room and put the cups on the table. 'Sorry I took so long, Leo.' She didn't want to let on that she'd heard any of the previous conversation. It seemed wrong to hear private business between the brothers. It made her uncomfortable.

Leo grabbed a cup and took a drink, pushing the plate with the doughnuts on it towards her. 'Go on, dive in.' He looked down at the papers spread in front of him and gave a sad kind of smile. 'The income of the clinic has skyrocketed since you got here, Lexi. We're going to be able to support Olivia Fairchild's charity much more than I originally thought. I want you to know you are worth your weight in gold.'

Lexi bit into the doughnut, blowing her calorie count for the whole day. It was as if the whole conversation before hadn't happened. However hurt Leo must currently be feeling, he wasn't showing it.

But Leo was good at that. He'd switched from personal to professional mode in an instant.

It was up to her to do the same. No matter how hard she found it.

She pulled out the spreadsheet she was looking for. 'I'm glad you're happy, Leo. There's just a couple of other things we have to discuss.' She laid them out on the table and opened a laptop, which had Iain's interview loaded and ready to be released.

Leo's eyes focused on the first shot. Iain in his dark suit, white shirt and red tie, standing in front of the Hunter Clinic sign with his arms folded across his chest. He let out a laugh. 'Lexi Robbins. How did you manage to get that shot?'

She raised her eyebrows and tapped her nose. 'I have my ways. But I'll never tell.'

Leo leaned back in his chair as he watched, shaking his head in wonder as the video finished. 'Wow, Lexi. You've done a fantastic job.' He glanced outside. 'I'd better hire a new receptionist. Our phones are going to ring off the hook.'

She nodded. 'I think you'd better.'

'It goes out tonight?'

'Yes.'

'Does Iain know? He's very private. I'm surprised he agreed to shoot it.'

She gathered up her papers, a knowing smile on her face. 'Let me handle Iain. I am the PR person after all.'

Leo nodded and gave her an appreciative smile. 'You certainly are.'

Iain was deep in surgery. He was grafting skin taken from the thigh onto a patient's cheek. His registrar was driving him crazy with all the questions she was asking.

'But why did you select the thigh area?'

He took a deep breath under his mask. 'We looked at the other traditional areas. The skin on her arms was too freckly, the skin on her buttocks wasn't suitable to transfer to her face. The skin on her thigh was the best option.'

The registrar let out a little sigh. 'It just seems so odd. Most people are more conscious about skin cancers these days—particularly on the face. Why didn't she see about it sooner?'

'And why didn't you read the case notes?' Iain snapped.

There was silence in the theatre. He could sense the rest of the staff cringing but he was tired of this lazy registrar with her enquiring mind. She asked thousands of questions without once looking for the answers herself.

And what's worse was that this patient had seen her doctor. She'd seen several doctors, several times, none of whom had referred her to get a biopsy until it was too late. Her cancer could still be treated, but if she'd been referred the first time she'd worried about the pale brown mark on her face, the surgery she would have needed would have been minimal. A tiny scar. Rather than extensive surgery into the surrounding tissues that required a skin graft. And if the registrar had bothered to do her job she would have known all that.

He gritted his teeth. He was getting to the most important part. He'd just separated the epidermis and part of the dermis layer ready to transfer to the face. His first surgical steps had been to remove the cancer thoroughly, ensuring margins wide enough to capture all the cells but small enough to allow the best outcome for the patient. Stitching the graft into place required steady hands, tiny stitches and intense concentration.

Concentration had never been a problem for Iain before. But then again he'd never been in a relationship with Lexi Robbins before.

And something was bothering him. Even though he'd almost been upfront and honest with her, something wasn't right with Lexi.

She was busy doing her job and flying around the world, drumming up publicity for the clinic and the charities. He'd taken her back to Frank's twice and she'd enjoyed it just as much as the first time.

But something was still wrong. He could sense it. He could *feel* it.

But it had been so long since he'd felt something, he couldn't rely on his instincts.

It didn't matter that he did his best to try and build Lexi's confidence. It didn't matter that she seemed happy at work and happy in his company. There was still just *something*.

And he didn't know what.

But what made matters worse was that he had no idea why this bothered him so much. Lexi was getting under his skin. He'd told her right from the start that he didn't think he had anything to offer her. But even as he'd said the words he'd felt conflicted. He'd wanted to give her an out. A way to walk away with no commitment.

But he wasn't that type of guy. And Lexi wasn't that type of woman.

He snapped his attention back to his work. What was wrong with him? He never lost focus.

Twittering. The registrar was twittering in his ear again. He honestly couldn't stand it.

He turned to face her. 'What is it exactly that you don't understand now? Because right now I'm busy. Right now I'm trying my hardest to make sure I line up the skin edges perfectly to give the best possible outcome for this patient. If I make a mess of this, she'll be left with permanent scarring on her face. If I do it well, after a few months the scars will fade and although they won't be invisible they won't be very noticeable to the average person. So what do you suggest I do? Should I allow myself to be distracted by you? To answer every question that you should have researched before you set foot in my theatre? Or should I just ignore you and get on with the job?'

Even beneath the mask he could see her mouth was hanging open. He waited for a noise, a loud clearing of the throat from the anaesthetist or the theatre sister. That was the general sign from them that it was time for him to wind it back in.

But no. There was nothing. They were obviously as fed up with the registrar as he was. She started to speak—to splutter behind her mask. 'But I'm here to—'

'No.' Iain held up the needle and suture that was in his hand. He shook his head. 'Just no.' He pointed towards the door and after a few seconds she stormed out in a huff.

There was nothing ominous about the silence that fell in the theatre. He could almost hear the collective sigh of relief.

Most of the time he was criticised for his directness. Today wasn't going to be one of those days.

He gave a smile as he looked over at the theatre sister. 'Now, where were we?'

She gave an almost approving nod. 'We were about to make Mrs Abbott look beautiful again, Iain. So let's get on with it.'

With the theatre quiet, he finished within an hour. He nodded at the theatre sister. 'The notes I write will be pretty extensive. I want to take these stitches out myself. I also want the dressing left in place until tomorrow and I want to be there when it comes off. I think Mrs Abbott will be a bit shocked and I want a bit of time to reassure her.'

'No problem, Iain. I'll pass that on to the ward staff. What's wrong with you these days?' She gave him a teasing smile. 'I thought you were returning to form earlier, but it seems someone has affected your bedside manner.' She was in her late fifties and had worked with Iain for the past two years. She was one of the few who could get away with saying that.

He peeled off his mask, gown and gloves, ignoring her last statement. 'I'm also going to write up some notes about moisturiser and massage for Mrs Abbott's post-op recovery treatment. Can you give me five minutes?'

But the theatre sister wasn't finished with Iain. She brushed past him, peeling off her own mask with a big smile on her face. 'So, are you going to tell me her name?'

On one hand he was amused, but this kind of light-hearted banter wasn't normal for Iain in

Theatre. He knew that they called him the grizzly bear behind his back.

'I've no idea what you're talking about.' He smiled. Then leaned over as he started to re-scrub his hands. 'And if I catch you speculating about me you'll get a whiff of anaesthetic gas,' he added wickedly.

'I think after all these years I'm probably immune. But do your worst, Iain. I'll find out.' She tapped the side of her nose. 'I always do.'

Iain finished washing and walked through to the changing rooms, dumping his scrubs and pulling his suit out of the locker. He was due back at Harley Street within an hour.

Was he really worried about anyone finding out about him and Lexi?

He wasn't sure. It wasn't a position he'd been in before. And he hadn't even discussed it with Lexi. He wasn't sure how she would feel about other people knowing about their relationship. It wouldn't make much difference to the staff at Kate's—most of them didn't know Lexi well. But the staff at the Hunter Clinic? That could be different. He would have to talk to her about it.

His pager went off as he fastened his tie. He frowned as he glanced at the number. His secretary rarely paged him unless it was an emergency. Carol Kennedy, the television presenter he'd performed surgery on a few weeks ago. Everything had been going so well. Lexi had even interviewed her again as she'd recovered. Carol wanted to use the film to show people what she'd been through and that there was light at the end of the tunnel.

Iain headed over to the nearest phone. If something was wrong with Carol he wanted to deal with it straight away. He never left his patients waiting. Never.

CHAPTER TEN

LEXI LOOKED AT her phone for the third time. *Need to talk to you later.*

What did that mean? Her stomach had been churning ever since Iain had sent the message late that afternoon. She'd tried to call him back but he hadn't been answering his phone and his grim secretary had only told her that there was an emergency with a patient.

It was after eight now. Surely he would be home by now? She rang the doorbell and let her stomach do some flip-flops while she waited for an answer.

Iain answered the door. He hadn't had time to change out of his suit. He looked tired, but smiled when he saw her.

'Hey, Lexi, I was just about to call you.'

She felt a little surge of relief. 'What happened?'

He held open the door and gestured for her to come inside.

Lexi stepped into his house. 'Is it someone I know?'

He nodded. 'It's Carol Kennedy. She had some haemorrhaging. I had to take her back to Theatre.'

'Oh, no. What happened?' She walked through to the kitchen and started emptying the bag on the kitchen table.

Iain gave a rueful smile as he picked up the crusty loaf she'd just unpacked. 'One of these. Or something similar.' He shook his head. 'She'd been warned about what to eat but thought she was doing better and could manage something she enjoyed. Unfortunately her throat wasn't completely healed.'

Lexi stared at the bread in his hand. 'Wow. I never knew a crusty loaf could cause damage to a throat.'

'Not normally. But after delicate throat surgery you have to be careful what you eat.' He picked up the cheese, pickle and cold ham she'd set on the table. 'Are we having a picnic tonight?'

Lexi smiled. 'I can't really cook. I try—but there's a real danger of food poisoning. So I decided not to even try.' She held up her hands. 'I don't want you to start getting false expectations about me.'

He crossed the room and put his hands on her hips. 'Oh, I've no false expectations about you, Lexi. You meet every single one of my expectations.'

'I do, do I?' She raised herself up on her toes and wound her hands around his neck. There it was. The picture still sitting on the window ledge. How could she have expected anything different? Of course the picture of Bonnie would still be there. There were pictures of her scattered throughout the house.

So why did it make her stomach curl so much? Bonnie wasn't here any more. And there was no question she had Iain's undivided attention. So why didn't it feel as if it was enough?

His hands were working their way around to her stomach. He still hadn't mentioned her abdominal scar. She'd already told him she'd had surgery as a child, maybe he just didn't want to pry.

It was still there. It was still eating away at her. The fact that Iain would eventually want a family of his own—one she couldn't provide. This was a fling. This was a fleeting event. And she had to keep reminding herself about that. Otherwise she could end up being seriously hurt.

Iain was paying particular attention to her neck. And their feet were moving slowly but surely in the direction of the bedroom. She pushed all the other thoughts from her mind. It was time to focus on the here and now because for the next few hours Iain was hers and hers alone.

And that was just the way she liked him.

Iain's pager sounded first thing in the morning with a shriek that made Lexi sit bolt upright in bed.

Iain's hand was on the phone in seconds, dialling in the number and listening for a few minutes. It couldn't be good. The only words he muttered were expletives.

'What's wrong?'

He shook his head. 'Can you spare some time today?'

She wrinkled her brow, trying not to think about the appointments she had, the calls to return and the final edits she had to do. 'I can try. What's wrong?'

'It's Carol Kennedy.'

'Did she have a bad night? Does she have post-op complications?'

Iain blew out a stream of air. 'Of the worst kind. Someone has blabbed to the media. One of the tabloids has been on the phone to Kate's, wanting a statement.'

Lexi cringed. 'Oh, no. Carol wanted the time to break the story herself. I've nearly finished editing the interview we did together. It's great. She comes across exactly as she is in real life, a woman with compassion and concern.'

'Well, by tomorrow she will be headline news on every front page.'

'Poor Carol. That's exactly what she didn't want.' Lexi put her head into her hands. 'I wonder...'

'Wonder what?'

Lexi stood up and walked around the bed. 'I hate to ask my parents for anything but if I could speak to my father, he has a show lined up for tonight. I could speak to him about screening Carol's interview.' She couldn't stop pacing. 'My father is quite mercenary. The thought of breaking the story would probably appeal to him.'

Iain nodded. Normally he would have hated anything like this but Carol had made her wishes clear. She wanted to break things on her terms. 'Can you talk to Carol this morning? Ask her how she wants to handle things?'

Lexi nodded. 'I take it you're happy with her recovery?'

He was picking up his clothes, pulling on his trousers. 'I'll come with you.' He paused from fastening his trousers. 'You can come this morning, can't you?'

Lexi nodded. She was Head of PR at the Hunter Clinic and this could rapidly turn into a PR nightmare. Everything else would have to wait. Including another viewing of the perfect interview with Iain. She'd watched it constantly since they'd filmed it. He was perfect. Just like a film star. And as soon as he opened his mouth and that Scottish accent came out— along with the slightly shaggy hair, good looks and toned body—he was going to be a sensation. The commercial had been let loose on the media last night. Neither of them had had time to think about it then—other priorities had taken over. She reached over and grabbed her phone. Dead as a doornail.

Iain was tucking his shirt in. 'What's wrong?'

She waved the phone at him. 'Out of charge.'

He pointed to the nearby table. 'Mine's plugged in over there—use it.'

She moved across the room and plugged in her phone. It vibrated instantly and she felt as if her eyes were bugging out her skull. *Four hundred emails. Sixty messages. One hundred and thirty-two texts.* Was somebody dead?

Then a smile crept across her face as she opened the first email. Just as she'd predicted. The world at large loved Iain McKenzie. He was going to be the latest internet sensation. She could see him in the bathroom, brushing his teeth. Better not tell him now. He'd probably freak. She could save it till later.

She sat on the edge of the bed and dialled her father's number, sighing when it went straight to voicemail. 'Hi, Dad, it's Lexi. I've got a bit of news for you—and an exclusive interview. Can you give me a call back?'

She put on her clothes and washed her face, pulling her hair back in a clip. Ready in less than five minutes.

Iain smiled. 'Let's go and see what we can do to help Carol.'

Six hours later Lexi hadn't stopped. And she'd had no chance whatsoever to respond to all the emails, messages and texts. Carol was making a good recovery following her op the day before and had given approval for her interview to be used on Lexi's father's show that night. She'd also recorded a new segment saying how she wanted to raise awareness of the type of cancer she had, and to say that her hand had been forced by the media to reveal her diagnosis before she'd wished to. It was skilfully done. Lexi's father had jumped all over the story, delighted to have the breaking news.

But even though she'd essentially done him a favour, he'd hardly even acknowledged the part that Lexi had played. It was nothing new to her. The thing that astonished her was that she still felt a tiny modicum of hurt about her father's actions. Or lack of them. Still, she had enough on her plate right now.

As for Iain McKenzie—internet sensation—she was so glad the interview had gone out the day before. If the Hunter Clinic was going to hit the news it was better to do it on her own terms. In a matter of minutes the footage of the hunky Scotsman had gone viral—just like she'd suspected it would. The phones at the clinic were currently ringing off the hook.

It seemed like she wasn't the only one who found Iain attractive. The rest of the female population were inclined the same way.

Needless to say, Iain hadn't been impressed. When they got back to the Hunter Clinic the amount of couriers with deliveries had staggered them all. Agencies looking to represent him had sent champagne and designer suits. Department stores wanting to use him for their advertising campaigns had sent their entire men's ranges. Aftershaves, flowers, bottles of whisky, ties, shirts and mountains of underwear were all waiting for him in his over-stuffed office.

Iain looked as if he might explode, but Lexi smiled. This was exactly what she'd expected. Fabulous publicity for the clinic and its attached charities.

And as a plus point the bookings had soared.

Now, if only she could get him into a kilt…

CHAPTER ELEVEN

THE SILVER ENVELOPE was lying on her desk, the courier logo across the top. She picked it up and stared at it. Who on earth was this from?

'When did this arrive?' She walked out of her office towards Rose, one of the secretaries.

Rose looked up and gave her a wary smile. 'About an hour ago. I signed for it. Is something wrong?'

Lexi shook her head. 'I don't think so.' She tore open the envelope and pulled the thick invitation out, letting out a little yelp when she realised what it was.

'Me? Me?' She couldn't believe it.

Rose jumped to her feet. 'Lexi? Lexi? Is something wrong?'

'What? Oh, no. Everything is wonderful!' She gave a little spin, waving the invitation above her head. 'I've been nominated for a PR award;

one of the biggest awards in PR!' She let out an excited squeal, 'I can't believe it. I've dreamed about this since I was at university. Every year we used to study the people who'd been nominated. I can't believe I'm one of them.'

The secretary gave a smile. 'Well, congratulations. That's fabulous news. For you, and for the clinic. Do you want me to let Leo know? He'll be thrilled for you.'

'What? Oh, yes. Thanks very much.' She kept the invitation close to her chest lest someone try to snatch it away from her. It was hers. It was really hers.

She couldn't wipe the smile from her face. It felt too good.

Finally, recognition for the job that she loved. Recognition that someone, somewhere thought she was doing a good job. There were hundreds of nominations for the PR award every year, only a few making it to the final cut. A panel had studied her work closely after the nomination. Thank goodness she hadn't known about that beforehand, it would have made her break out in a cold sweat.

She walked down the corridor, heading towards Iain's office. He was the first person she wanted to tell. Was that weird? The other people she really wanted to know were her parents. But she didn't want to have to tell them herself. She didn't want to give them the ability to shrug off her news as if it was meaningless.

If she kept quiet long enough, the press would eventually break the story. Maybe her parents would pay more attention then? Was it wrong to know that her parents would be more likely to celebrate her success if it brought them good promo?

She shook the thought from her head.

'What are you looking so happy about?' Iain had crept up behind her, placed his hands on her hips and was escorting her into his office, shutting the door with his foot.

'This!' Lexi spun around, waving the silver envelope.

Iain smiled, leaned against the door and folded his arms. 'Okay, you got me. What is it?'

She couldn't help it. She started jumping up and down on the spot. Even wearing stilettos she couldn't contain her excitement. 'It's such a big a nomination. I can't believe I got it. I can't believe I got nominated. I don't care about winning. Just getting nominated is so, so fabulous!'

'You finalled? Really? That's brilliant! I knew you would!'

He bent down and kissed her thoroughly. His kisses took her breath away. The feel of his hands on her body made her forget everything else—including the fact they were in the clinic.

Well, not quite everything. In the currently messy recesses of her mind a little alarm bell had gone off.

She pulled back. 'You don't seem surprised.'

'Maybe I believe in you. Maybe I value the work that you do. Maybe I think the world should know how good you are. Look at the fabulous job you did with Carol Kennedy. Everyone is talking about her. Everyone is talking about the warning signs of cancer.'

She felt a little warmth spread through her chest. 'It was you, wasn't it? You nominated me for this award?'

It was an incredible feeling. A swelling of

pride. Something she rarely experienced in this life—not with the parents she had.

It made her feel special. It made her feel worthy. All things she'd spent this life striving for. And in a few short weeks Iain had made that happen for her. There was no getting away from the fact that she could happily spend the rest of her life like this. Happily spend the rest of her life with Iain—if only he didn't want kids so badly.

He touched her face. 'Of course I nominated you for the award. I've seen the hours you put in. I've seen the changes you've made in the last few months. The number of celebrity clients has gone through the roof. You know they're not my favourite kind, but if they help the clinic, and help with the charity work we can do, I can live with that.' He pulled her even closer. '*You* did this work, Lexi. *You* did. I just nominated you for the award. The panel scrutinised the work that you've done. They found it worthy to give you a place as a finalist. You should be proud of yourself. The work you've done here is amazing.'

The silver envelope was still trapped between

them, against the hard planes of his chest and the firm curves of her breasts. She looked down at it and smiled. 'I think this is all a ploy.'

'A ploy?' Iain arched his eyebrows.

'Definitely. You must know this invitation is for two people. You're trying to trick me into going out in public with you.' It was risky. It was more than risky. They hadn't let anyone at work know about their relationship. Everything had been kept tightly under wraps. This would blow things out of the water.

She felt her heart flutter in her chest. Beating much faster than it should. Didn't they have a special name for this? AF? Didn't this normally require medical treatment? Just as well she was in a doctor's arms.

She was pretending to breathe normally. Pretending that this was an everyday question. Pretending that she didn't feel sick asking it.

She could see Iain thinking. She could almost hear his brain ticking. Trying to decide what to tell her. Did he want to let her down gently? Because, frankly, that would kill her.

But just when she thought he was going to

break her heart, he leaned forward and gave her a kiss. It was lighter than before, a little more formal.

'It would be my pleasure to be your date. I think you'll knock them out.'

She tried not to let the hiss of relief from her lungs be audible. Her smile was back, pasted from one ear to the other. 'So,' she said as she wound her hands around his neck, 'what are my chances of getting you in a kilt?'

Lexi looked in the mirror and tried not to let her hand tremble as she took the large rollers from her hair. It fell in loose curls, just the way she'd wanted. Everything should be perfect.

But inside her chest her heart was pitter-pattering the fast beat of nerves. This wasn't about Iain. This wasn't about the award ceremony. This was about being *her*.

She shrugged the satin robe from her shoulders, immediately averting her eyes from the full-length mirror in front of her.

Her breasts were perfect. There was no denying the fantastic job her plastic surgeon had done. But although she liked them, she was still naturally shy about her body shape. She wasn't the kind of girl who'd ever go topless on a beach. She stepped into her pink satin underwear and fastened her bra around her back. There. Now she looked up.

Her hand rested on her stomach. The line of her panties didn't quite hide the scar on her abdomen. The scar that Iain had never asked about.

Just that thought sent the hairs on the back of her neck standing on end. It was inevitable. At some point he would ask and at some point she would tell him. And that time was creeping closer with every day.

Within a few seconds she'd pulled her dress over her head. Better, much better. Now her body was covered. It was almost as if she'd pulled on her suit of armour.

The dress enhanced her shape, covered all the parts of her she wanted covered. And let her move past the things she didn't want to think about.

She sat down in the chair and fastened her jewel-encrusted sandals. She could almost see the headlines. The Lexi Robbins who appeared in the press was so different from the Lexi Robbins who stared at her in the mirror.

These last few weeks had been easier. She was little more relaxed. A little more confident. She fastened her earrings. Iain. He was the difference here.

He never failed to compliment her. He never failed to tell her how good he thought she looked.

She looked up again. She liked the pale pink and silver dress. Not too much cleavage, not too much leg. She was comfortable in it. Some people might call her a princess in it.

Too bad that wasn't how she felt.

She fixed a smile on her face. There. That was better.

Iain would be here soon. Her stomach gave a little flip. She pushed the nerves away and finished her make-up with some rose-coloured lipstick. It wasn't dark enough, she would need a second coat. That could wait until Iain was here.

She flicked the switch on the radio and tuned in to some classic tunes. Anything to distract her right now. Anything to take her mind off the sea of cameras that would be waiting for her in the next hour.

Iain would be right next to her. And with him there, everything would be all right—wouldn't it?

Iain knocked on her door, the London wind whistling about his knees. This wind was for amateurs. If he was in Edinburgh right now the wind would have his kilt dancing somewhere around his ears. It had been a long time since he'd taken his kilt out of its carrier. A very long time. He used to love wearing his kilt on special occasions. Then again, he used to love going out—something he rarely did in London.

Lexi opened the door and let out a squeal. 'You did it! You wore the kilt!'

Her face was a picture. For a second he was transfixed by the sparkle in her eyes and broadest of smiles.

Until he became distracted by the floaty pale pink chiffon of her dress. A sleeveless dress with broad straps and a cross-over bodice, scattered with silver sequins that skimmed down across her hips. Her waist was accentuated by a pale pink ribbon cinched around it, giving her a perfect hourglass shape. The dress skimmed her knees. There was nothing revealing about it. Nothing to attract undue attention. But the way it clung to her body and accentuated her curves was attention-grabbing enough for Iain. That, along with how the dress rippled in the wind, made her look like a butterfly, waiting to be captured.

She'd left her blonde hair in loose curls over her shoulders, there was a light tan on her skin, and her feet were encased in red-soled silver sparkling shoes. She'd never looked so beautiful.

'Wow, Lexi. Just wow. You don't need to win the award tonight. No one will be able to take their eyes off you.'

She waved her hand and picked up her evening purse. 'Sure they won't. They'll be more interested in the free food and free bar.' She paused in front of the mirror and applied some more pink lipstick, giving him a cheeky wink. 'I, on the other hand, will spend the whole night wondering if you're a true Scotsman or not.'

'Wanna find out now?'

'Naughty.' She batted his hands away, picking up the silver invitation and tucking it into her bag.

His hands caught her around the waist. There was no way he was leaving here without a kiss. He bent forward and nibbled at her neck, catching the aroma of her trademark perfume. It sent his pulse racing. What kind of underwear did she have on under that beautiful dress?

'So, Lexi. Make me pass out with shock at the price of that dress. You look stunning.'

'This?' She shook her head. 'I bought it on the high street. I'm sure the fashion press will have plenty to say about that tomorrow.' She lifted her leg and extended her sparkling shoe towards him. 'These, however, would probably make me remortgage my house.'

'Really? Shoes?' He stared for a few moments. Sure, they were pretty. And they matched the dress. But crazy money—on shoes?

He shook his head and watched as she fastened some glittering earrings on her lobes. 'Are you ready?'

She took one last glance in the mirror then picked up her bag. Her hands were trembling slightly. Lexi Robbins was nervous. He couldn't believe it. She looked a million dollars and her work spoke for itself. Just about every newspaper in the country had covered Carol Kennedy's story after her interview had appeared on Lexi's father's show.

Carol had shown great courage, though not without a tear or two. She'd let the cameraman film her drains being removed, the initial scars. The post-op complications. Every time she spoke there was a tiny waver in her voice that was overcome by her courage and the message that she wanted to share with others. It was media gold and everyone knew it.

The only thing that had irked Iain had been the glossing over of Lexi's role. Her name had appeared in the credits of her father's show, but very little had been said about the work she had done. That was part of the reason he'd nominated her for the award. He wanted the world to know about the sterling work that she had done.

And that was without mentioning the current

waiting list of clients he'd had since his interview for the Hunter Clinic had exploded all over
the media. If it had been anyone but Lexi, he
might have been annoyed to be in the public
eye. But it would only be for a few weeks then
they would move on to someone else. Or so he
hoped.

The flashlights exploded as they stepped from
the car outside the prestigious London hotel. For
the first time in his life Iain could hear people
shouting his name, vying for his attention. And
he didn't like it. He didn't like it one little bit.

'Dr Sexy! Look over here first!'

It didn't help that the hotel had laid a red carpet outside and set up sponsorship banners for
photographers. Iain kept his arm tightly around
Lexi's waist and tried to steer her directly inside.

'Lexi, are you dating Iain McKenzie? Is that
why you did the interview?'

'Lexi, where's the dress from?'

'Dr McKenzie, what's your relationship with
Lexi Robbins?'

He grimaced. Ignorant journalist. He was a
surgeon. He was Mr McKenzie, not Dr. And he

couldn't even begin to say what his intentions towards Lexi were—because he didn't know himself.

The hotel was stunning and after the first glass of champagne Lexi's nerves seemed to settle. She moved into professional PR mode, working the room, circulating and talking to everyone, without letting Iain leave her side.

After around half an hour he felt Lexi stiffen. He didn't even need to ask why. Her mother and father had entered the room to a round of applause. They moved through the crowd effortlessly. And after a few minutes' fascination he quickly came to the realisation that they were their own biggest fans.

They barely even glanced at their beautiful daughter and Iain could feel the fire surge in his belly.

Lexi was pretending not to notice. She was smiling and talking politely to those around her, even though it was blindingly obvious to the whole room that her parents hadn't even taken the time to acknowledge her.

She pressed her hand on Iain's arm. 'You'll

need to excuse me a minute, Iain, I need to check my make-up.' He could see unshed tears hiding behind her eyes. She needed a little time out. A little space to collect herself.

'No problem,' he muttered, watching her cross the room in her fluttering dress. As soon as she was out of sight he walked directly over to the bar, where her father was ordering champagne.

He held out his hand. 'Steve Robbins? I'm Iain McKenzie. I'm here with your daughter tonight.'

Lexi's father frowned then switched into false mode and shook Iain's hand. He could tell the man wasn't the least bit interested, but Iain hadn't even started yet.

Lexi's mother sidled up to the bar in a blue silk sheath dress, her eyes watching her own reflection in the mirror behind the bar.

'I nominated Lexi for the award this evening. She's done some really fantastic work at the Hunter Clinic.'

Penelope Crosby lifted her eyebrows. He could tell it was because the conversation wasn't directly focused on her. What a sad woman. But she couldn't deter him.

'Lexi has raised over a hundred thousand pounds in the last few weeks for the charity work of the clinic.'

'Charity work, huh?' Lexi's father shook his head. 'More likely lining the pockets of you and your colleagues.'

Iain stilled the fire in his belly. 'I don't need anyone else to line my pockets. I probably earn more money than you do,' he shot back, without the slightest hint of embarrassment. 'I think you should appreciate the wonderful job that your daughter does. She gave you that breakthrough a few weeks ago with *my* patient Carol Kennedy. None of that filming would have taken place if I hadn't agreed to it. And the only reason Carol spoke to Lexi was because Lexi was genuinely concerned about her and showed her some compassion.' He took a drink from his whisky sitting on the bar. 'A trait that obviously doesn't run in the family.'

Lexi's mother looked horrified. She'd spent her life with people fawning over her and obviously wasn't used to be spoken to like that.

Iain finished his whisky. 'Tell me, Mr Robbins, exactly how much of a rating boost did that interview give your flagging show? And have you thanked your daughter for it yet?'

Lexi's father's face started to turn beetroot. 'How dare you?'

'Oh, I dare.'

'Who do you think you are?'

'I think I'm the person who knows your daughter is beautiful, inside and out.' He replaced his glass on the bar. 'I'm the person who thinks she works hard and deserves recognition for the job that she does. That's who I think I am.'

The beetroot colour was settling on Lexi's father's face. It was turning to an embarrassed dark glow.

'It's such a pity that Lexi still looks for your approval.' He paused, there was so much more he could say here. But the truth was it really wasn't his business. He'd probably already overstepped the mark.

It was time to leave her parents' company. Lexi's mother had stopped being horrified and was back to checking her reflection in the mirror behind the bar again. And as beautiful as her reflection was, she had nothing on Lexi.

She didn't have Lexi's heart. Or Lexi's soul. She didn't have any of the compassion or humility that Lexi showed. She was so self-centred. Iain couldn't bear to in her company a second longer.

He watched as Lexi came out of the ladies and gave her a wave. He didn't want her to come over here. To listen to the indifference of her parents. He gave them a quick glance. 'I just want you to know that I'm proud of Lexi, even if you aren't.'

But no matter what he thought, Lexi was on her way over, with a tilt to her chin that proved she was ready.

She walked over, sliding her hand into his and smiling as he gave it a squeeze. She angled her cheek as her father gave her a kiss. 'Congratulations on your nomination, Lexi.' His eyes shot to Iain. 'You know that we are proud of you.' Her mother hadn't moved from the bar, almost as if she was waiting for her cue.

And there it was. 'Lexi, darling, you look wonderful!' She stepped over from the bar with her arms in the air, her blue sheath-style dress barely allowing her to move. Her arms closed around her daughter's neck just as there was the flash of a camera.

Iain cringed. It was obvious she'd orchestrated the whole thing. Lexi was spun around and positioned between her parents just as one of the photographers from a national magazine appeared. 'Oh, perfect!' the photographer shouted. 'I don't know who is more beautiful, mother or daughter!'

It was pretty obvious to Iain, but he waited a few moments as the photographer positioned them all exactly as he wanted them and snapped away. Lexi's mother spent most of the time throwing back her head and laughing—obviously the way she wanted to be captured on film. When the photographer nodded that he was finished, Lexi slid out from under her parents' grasp and took a few steps back to Iain.

He bent to give her a kiss. Raspberries. She tasted of raspberries. 'Let's go and mingle,' he said to her, guiding her away from her parents. She didn't even glance in their direction. They'd moved on to speak to another TV personality with barely a few words to their daughter. And he could tell from the tension in her body and the sheen in her eyes that she hadn't quite collected herself yet.

He glanced at his watch and scoped out the bar on the other side of the room. 'How about a little cocktail before they announce the awards?'

She jerked to attention. 'Is it that time already?' She looked stunned, almost as if she'd forgotten why she was there. He loved that about her.

They made their way to the bar and Iain grabbed the cocktail menu. 'What's your favourite? Vodka? Rum? Whisky?'

She wrinkled her nose. 'Whisky cocktail? Yuck.' Her eyes ran down the menu. 'I'll have a raspberry daiquiri.'

He smiled. 'I should have guessed. You taste of raspberries already.'

She smiled and ran her tongue along her lips. Boy, just that tiny action could drive him crazy. He gave their order at the bar and waited while the bartender mixed the frozen cocktails. Then they stood quietly for the next half-hour, his arm around her waist as they drank their cocktails.

Then the lights in the room dimmed and the compère appeared on the stage, giving a short presentation about the awards and past recipients. The PR award was one of the first to be announced. One by one the nominees appeared on screen, along with a presentation about their work. Then Lexi's face appeared on the screen ahead of them.

She flinched. 'Oh, no. I don't like my face in high definition.' She burrowed her face into his shoulder. 'It shows all the blemishes.'

Iain took a deep breath. There it was again. The fact that Lexi didn't see what he did. On the screen ahead of him he saw a beautiful fresh-faced woman. Long eyelashes around clear blue eyes, luscious pink lips and long blonde curls. She could out-supermodel her mother any day of the week.

He slipped his finger underneath her chin and tilted her head up towards his. 'Trust me, Lexi, there are no blemishes.' He kissed her again, tasting the raspberries still on her lips and pulling her closer to him.

Clapping broke out around them and they both broke apart.

'Is it over?' Lexi asked, her hands pressed against his chest. She started to clap, even though he knew neither of them had heard the announcement of the winner. A face flashed up on the screen of one of the male nominees who worked for a newly opened fashion chain. They watched as he walked up on stage in his sharp suit and gave his acceptance speech.

Iain squeezed Lexi around her waist, his fingers catching the chiffon material and silver sequins beneath his hands. 'You were robbed,' he whispered in her ear.

She shook her head firmly. 'No, I wasn't. He's done a good job. He deserves it.' She kept clapping until he left the stage. 'I feel lucky to be nominated. I never thought I was going to win anyway, so I'm not disappointed.'

He could tell she meant it. Her generous spirit was still evident, showing grace in defeat. 'Well,

I'm disappointed for you. I thought you deserved to win.'

She stood on tiptoe and kissed his cheek. 'Thank you, Iain. That's the nicest thing anyone's said to me all night.' She squeezed his hand. 'What do you say we get out of here?'

She had that gleam in her eyes. The ones that could send a sweep of sensation down to his toes, igniting all the parts of his body it needed to.

'Let's go now.' Even he could recognise how husky his voice sounded. He only had one thing on his mind.

'Give me five minutes to visit the ladies before we go.' And before he could even answer she'd swept away and ducked into the nearest ladies room. All he could see was the flutter of her pale pink dress around her legs.

It was more than he needed.

CHAPTER TWELVE

LEXI STOOD IN front of the mirror and re-applied her rose-coloured lipstick. Her face was flushed. But it was excitement. Excitement over what would happen next with Iain.

He'd been fabulous with her tonight. Supporting her with her parents and keeping her close during the award announcements. But she wasn't disappointed at all about not winning.

Truth was, she already felt as if she'd won because Iain had nominated her and brought her here tonight.

She took one final glance in the mirror. The dress he'd admired so much was nice. Much nicer than some of the dresses tonight that were ten times the price. It just went to show that pricier wasn't always better.

She gave a little smile then walked back outside to meet Iain.

Her eyes swept the room. He was only a few feet away, talking to some man in a dark suit.

A voice breathed in her ear, 'Well, what do we have here?'

Her stomach turned over, thankfully not all over her dress. A blast from the past. And one she certainly didn't welcome.

She spun round in her sparkling shoes. 'Jack, what an unpleasant surprise.'

Jack Parker was standing in front of her, his arm around a buxom blonde who looked as if she was being strangled by her bright blue dress. How on earth she'd managed to contain her oversized breasts in a dress two sizes too small was anybody's guess. His tie was askew and his hair rumpled. What a surprise—Jack Parker was drunk.

He leaned forward and she got the whiff of alcohol on his breath. Any closer and he could anaesthetise her.

'I saw you up on the screen. Close up doesn't do you much good, does it?'

She took a deep breath. 'I could say the same about you, Jack,' she shot back.

He raised one eyebrow. What had she ever found attractive about this guy?

Her stomach was churning. He was saying out loud the thoughts that had sprung into her mind the second she'd seen her face on the screen. Jack Parker was still inside her head. Still circulating little horrible thoughts. It made her angry. It made her angry that she was still allowing him to influence her thoughts, and have a little bit of control over her life.

She ran her eyes up and down his rumpled suit. 'Did you pick that one straight up out of the garden after I dumped it there?'

His eyes narrowed. He wasn't used to Lexi standing up for herself. He wasn't used to it at all. She'd always found a way to try and avoid any arguments with him. Had spent most of her time trying to placate him. More fool her.

And for a time it had seemed his greatest pleasure was to make her cry. Well, not tonight.

Jack's drunken girlfriend swayed and turned to him. 'What's she talking about, baby? I thought you dumped her?'

Her hand rested on his chest. There was something vaguely familiar about her. Lexi's eyes dropped to her obviously over-implanted breasts. Of course, she was a glamour model. But her breasts stood out like sore thumbs. Lexi could tell just by looking that they were obviously too large for her slim frame. And her implants had been placed over her chest muscles instead of under, causing obvious ridge marks at the tops of breasts. Oh, dear. Even Lexi could tell this woman would need reconstructive surgery at some point. Had Jack made her do that?

She could feel the fire building in her belly. On any other day if she'd seen Jack Parker she would have ducked and hidden. She didn't like conflict. She didn't like attention being on herself. It didn't matter that she'd picked up the courage to throw him out. Even one glance of Jack brought back the overwhelming surge of not being good enough. It brought back the seeds of doubt and the memories of his cruel words and actions.

She looked across the room. She wasn't panicking—she was just looking for some reassurance. Iain was still in conversation with another man just a few feet away. He obviously hadn't realised anything was wrong.

These last few weeks with Iain had given her some new-found confidence. She felt appreciated. She felt respected. She felt...loved?

Something she'd never felt before. Either with Jack or her parents. Her aunt was the only person who'd ever shown her love.

It was a startling realisation. It almost made her feel giddy.

Jack was wrinkling his nose at her, mumbling under his breath. She couldn't stand him. She couldn't stand to be in the same place as him. Even now he treated her with disdain. How dared he?

She straightened her shoulders, gave a smile to his girlfriend and extended her hand. 'Pleasure to meet you. I'm Lexi Robbins. Jack's never had any manners and that's obviously not changed.' As she took the action she was aware of Jack's eyes on her bust. Even though she was perfectly happy with her figure, it could clearly never compete with his new girlfriend's. And she'd never want to. She couldn't imagine the health problems the woman was likely to have in the future.

The blonde's eyes widened as she took the hand in front of her and gave it a limp shake. Jack was spluttering over his drink but Lexi ignored him.

'Brandy,' she slurred.

Brandy. It figured.

'And just so we're clear, you're wrong,' Lexi continued. 'I dumped Jack. In fact, I threw his clothes out of our flat and changed the locks. That's because he's a weasel. You'd do well to remember that.'

The colour started to rise in Jack's face. 'Rubbish, Lexi. That's rubbish. You were too boring for me.' He glanced back at Brandy, obviously desperate to save face. 'In more ways than one. And, obviously, not pretty enough.' He pulled Brandy closer to him. Was that to reassure her? Or to stop himself from swaying?

'Get a life, Jack,' Lexi sighed, and gave a shake of her head. 'You're not worth it. Not for a second.'

She spun on her heel and walked back into the

ladies. She didn't want to let him have a minute more of her time. She didn't want all the little self-doubts to find their way into her mind and thoughts again. She stood for a second in front of the mirror, taking a few deep breaths.

She wanted to get of here. She needed to get out of here. She needed to find Iain and stick to their original plan. The original plan that made her knees quiver and her heart race.

The door banged behind her and before she could even lift her head to look at who had entered she was grabbed roughly from behind. There was no time to think. No time to act.

She was pushed against the wall, the cold tiles pressing against her back. Jack had one hand on her shoulder, the other around her throat.

She tried to move her arms, her hands, but his full weight was on her. He leaned forward. 'Who do you think you are? Don't you dare speak to me like that.'

She turned her head away, trying to avert the smell of alcohol that was coming from his breath.

'Look at me!' he growled.

She closed her eyes tightly and shook her head. 'Get off me, Jack. This is a public restroom, any minute now someone will walk in and see what you're doing.'

He snarled. 'Who's going to stop me?' He lifted one hand and waved it around, laughing as she took the opportunity to try and escape his grasp. 'There's no one here but you and me.'

He pressed his hand back to her body, this time reaching up and squeezing her breast. 'You should be thanking me. Thanking me for telling you to get some shape.' He gave another little laugh. 'But you'll never compare to Brandy.'

She winced under his grasp. Jack had never been physical with her in the past, but the amount of alcohol he'd consumed—along with his bad temper—made her glad things had never been like this.

She opened her eyes and looked him straight in the eye. She didn't even notice the door open in the background. She was too focused on her task.

Fight or flight. The surge of adrenaline powered through her body.

'That's just it Jack, I don't want to be anything like Brandy.' She leaned towards him, ignoring the stench of alcohol. 'But you're right. It's just you and me.'

She lifted her knee and hammered it straight into his groin. His reaction was instant. He released her and crumpled to the floor, clutching at his groin.

She stepped over him in her fluttering dress. 'Don't you ever put a hand on me again.'

There was a movement beside her. A dark flash of something. It took her a few seconds to register that Iain had appeared.

And she didn't recognise the expression on his face. She'd never seen Iain angry before.

He lifted Jack clean off the floor and slammed him against the white tiles where he'd just held Lexi. If she'd thought Jack had been snarling at her before, he'd had nothing on Iain. The steam was practically coming out of his ears.

'Don't you dare touch Lexi ever again.' His

eyes flicked to Lexi. 'Are you okay? Do you want to press charges?'

She shook her head. She just wanted to get out of there.

Jack had shrunk back against the tiles. He wasn't so brave when confronted by a six-foot-four angry Scotsman.

Iain spun him round, grabbing him by the collar of his shirt and the back of his trousers. Jack's feet were skimming the floor as Iain thrust him towards the door. A woman opened it and walked in, letting out a little shriek when she saw the two men in the ladies. Wordlessly she held the door open as Iain escorted Jack from the building.

He was quietly efficient about it, stopping only once to pull out his card and hand it to an astonished Brandy. 'Chronic back pain?'

She nodded in a stunned silence.

'Come and see me some time and we'll chat about what's best for you.'

Jack was strangely silent. Any time his steps seemed to hesitate Iain just lifted him clean off the floor to help him on his way. They reached the outer door and Iain ejected him down the steps.

Lexi cringed as he tumbled down them into a puddle outside. Iain stood next to her and slid his arm around her waist. He pointed at Jack. 'I'm warning you, Jack. I don't want you within fifty feet of Lexi.'

He turned and steered her down the street, away from the event and towards the footpath to the Thames. She could see his hand still shaking slightly. She knew it was with rage. But she wasn't scared around Iain. He was a big man, who could probably intimidate anyone in his vicinity. But the rage would never be aimed at her. She felt secure with him beside her. She felt safe around Iain. But that wasn't all she felt and that's what was bothering her.

His arms swept around her as he laid her coat across her shoulders. She hadn't even realised he'd picked up her coat for her. She pulled it around her and slid her arms into the sleeves. March was cold in London, it wouldn't do to be without her coat.

Iain pulled her closer as they walked along

in silence. Her brain was whirring with a million thoughts that she just couldn't even begin to compute.

Even though she'd tried her very best, the tiny little seeds of doubt were creeping into her brain. Seeds that Jack had initially planted and which had sprouted and grown. She'd thought she'd dealt with those. She'd thought she'd doused them with the weedkiller they deserved.

But seeing Jack again had brought them all flooding back, no matter how hard she tried. Except this time the thoughts weren't about Jack. This time the seeds of doubt were all about her and Iain.

It was ridiculous. Iain had only ever treated her with respect. He'd never mocked her body—quite the opposite, in fact. He'd never let her think she wasn't good enough.

So why were thoughts like that circulating in her brain?

Why would Iain be interested in someone like her? She wasn't a supermodel. She was clever but not a genius. She'd done a good job with the publicity and charitable donations for the clinic.

A horrible startling realisation crept over her. Maybe he was just trying to keep her sweet? Trying to make sure the Hunter Clinic was known around the world?

No. Iain would never be like that.

He'd almost fought against the attraction between them. And he'd been more than supportive regarding her parents and her surgery.

So why was a whole host of doubts creeping into her head?

She leaned against him a little as they walked down the path to the Thames. It was beautiful at this time of night. The path next to the dark river twinkled with little lights leading towards the brightly lit Tower Bridge. If you wanted to find a romantic location in London at night, you really couldn't do better.

It was cold enough to still see their breath in the air. Cold enough to have an excuse to snuggle closer.

But Lexi felt changed from before. The feelings of uncertainty were making her feel differently.

There was no getting away from it. She'd fallen

hard for Iain. Hard and fast. She'd shared things with him in a way she'd never shared with anyone at all.

And he'd shared with her too.

Only not enough.

A wave of cold air swept over her body, sending a little shiver across her skin.

That was it. That was what was wrong.

She turned and looked at his profile as they walked along the path. She could almost sense he was in as much turmoil as she was. They weren't talking. They were simply holding each other and walking. But at some point they were going to reach the crescendo of what was happening between them. Reach the tipping point.

Her velvet coat wasn't giving her any warmth right now. The cold feeling wouldn't leave her.

Iain had told her about his wife. He'd told her about his babies. It must have truly broken his heart. But there was more. There was more that he hadn't told her.

And if they really had a chance at a relationship, she had to know what it was.

It was haunting them. It was a dark storm-cloud permanently hanging over their heads. Because no matter how charming, how happy Iain seemed to be, the only time the shadows really disappeared from his eyes was when they were making love.

And it wasn't enough. It wasn't enough for her any more.

Her stomach twisted. Iain still didn't know. He still didn't know about the fact she'd had a hysterectomy and couldn't have children. He'd accepted her story about being injured by a horse as a young girl and had never questioned her scarring.

This was a man who had wanted a family. A family that she couldn't give him.

Maybe his past experience would have put him off. Maybe he would tell her that he could never go through that again. It was a possibility. But it was one they had never discussed.

She had to get things out in the open. *They* had to get things out in the open.

She wanted honesty from him. She wanted full disclosure. No matter what it was.

Iain McKenzie had rapidly turned into her

dream man. But his constant reassurance and support was about to backfire. Her new-found confidence made her realise what she wanted in this life.

She didn't want to be a bystander. She didn't want to be known as someone's daughter. She wanted to be loved for who she was. She didn't want things to be hidden from her. And she didn't want to have to hide anything from him.

And while she didn't mind the photos of Bonnie in Iain's house, she didn't know what they meant for them. Would Iain ever lose the shadows in his eyes? It was a miserable, selfish thought but she couldn't compete with a ghost. If Bonnie still had the biggest part of his heart then Lexi shouldn't be here. She couldn't allow herself to be second best. No matter how cruel it might seem. She deserved better.

If this relationship had any chance at all, it was time to take the big step.

She stopped walking. 'Iain, we need to talk.'

He turned to face her immediately and she sensed him hesitate as he drew in a deep breath.

Had he heard the tremble in her voice? Or was he noticing the sheen in her eyes?

Then, before she had a chance to say anything, his arms swept her in and his lips descended on hers.

It was as if all the rage and pent-up frustration was being translated into his passion for her. His arms cradled her, but his lips devoured her. Their teeth clashed as his tongue slid into her mouth. There was no mistaking how he felt about her.

And there was no mistaking how she felt about him.

He pulled back, breathless, his arms gently releasing their grip on her waist. In this dim light his dark chocolate eyes looked almost black. Darker than the bottom of his soul.

He'd blindsided her with that kiss. For a second all her rational thoughts had vanished, as had the sinking feeling in her heart.

They stood together next to the Thames, their warm breath visible in the cold air as her rapid heartbeat quietened to a mild canter.

She had to stay focused.

She had to think of the future.

Hers. And Iain's. She needed more than his passion. She needed more than his protectiveness.

She needed his heart and his soul.

His hands rested on her hips. 'Lexi, I'm sorry about my behaviour. When I saw him touching you like that—assaulting you—I saw red. It just descended all around me. I couldn't wait to get my hands on him. I couldn't wait to get him away from you. I didn't want him near you.'

There was tension in his words—as if he'd just taken himself back to the moment again. He thought she was angry. He thought she wanted to talk to him about the incident with Jack.

'I was filled with rage. I wanted to punch him senseless.'

She lifted her hand and put it on his chest. 'And I might have let you.'

He shook his head. 'But I never behave like that.' He squeezed his eyes shut for a moment then gave her a sorry smile. 'But, with hindsight, you seemed to have got the better of him yourself.'

She nodded. 'But that doesn't mean I didn't appreciate the help.' This wasn't the conversation she wanted to have. She didn't want to waste a second of her life talking about Jack Parker.

She could tell Iain was nervous. Maybe he was worried about how he'd manhandled Jack in front of her. But Jack Parker and his welfare was the last thing on her mind right now.

He knew something was wrong. Even though his hands were on her hips, he couldn't look her in the eye. They were fixed over her shoulder on Tower Bridge.

'I need to ask you something, Iain.'

'What is it?' His eyes had met hers now. He looked worried. For the first time since she'd known him he looked afraid. What did Iain have to be scared of?

Maybe she should start slowly.

'I need to ask you why. Why do you think you felt like that?'

Confusion swept his face. 'Why do you think? Because he touched you, because he assaulted you. He should never have laid a hand on you.'

She breathed in slowly through her nose. 'And

you didn't like that?' She was trying to be controlled. She was trying to be measured. Iain meant the world to her and she was going to have to be strong to do this.

'What about us?'

He stiffened, his shoulders pushing back and down, his body arching away from her. 'What do you mean, "What about us?"'

She ran her tongue along her lips. All of a sudden her mouth was instantly dry. She could do with some of the wine she'd refused at the award ceremony. She knew exactly what she was doing. Even if Iain didn't.

'Where do you think we are going, Iain?'

He shook his head. 'I don't understand. Where did this come from?' He reached up and touched her cheek. 'You know how I feel about you.'

She held her breath, trying not to turn her head towards his cheek. She had to stay strong.

'I care about you, Lexi. You know I do.'

Care.

A gentle word. A quiet word. A word without passion and without soul. Nothing like the passion he'd just shown her. Her heart could break in two right now.

Her gaze swept down to the wet street. Black, totally black. Just like the sensations that were coursing through her body.

'Care. It's an interesting choice of word.' Even she could hear how detached her voice sounded. How disappointed.

He wasn't looking at her again. She understood. He *couldn't* look at her. He couldn't give her any more. Put him on the spot and he just shut down.

This was pointless. She wanted more than Iain could ever offer her. It was time to walk away.

This was a disaster. This whole night had been a disaster and it was nothing to do with Lexi not winning the award.

She deserved better than him. He should have watched her more closely—kept an eye on her. Jack Parker would never have got his hands on her then. He shuddered to think what could have happened in there.

He hadn't been able to protect her. Just like he hadn't been able to protect his wife.

But now Lexi was asking him difficult questions. It would be so much easier to shrug them off and just continue as before. Their relationship was developing slowly. But he still couldn't be honest with her. He wasn't ready.

But her trembling lips were breaking his resolve—no matter how hard she was trying to hide them.

'I don't care about you, Iain.'

His head shot around to face her. 'What?'

She shook her head firmly as a single tear trailed down her cheek. She lifted her hand and pressed it against her chestbone. 'I love you. I didn't want to. I *don't* want to. But I can't help how I feel.' She looked at him with her big blue eyes. 'But I know you don't feel the same, Iain. I can tell. I can *feel* it.'

He opened his mouth to speak but she lifted her hand to stop him.

'Don't. Don't make this any harder than it already is. You can't share with me—not really. There are permanent shadows around your eyes.

The only time they vanish is when we make love. And it's not enough, Iain. It's not enough for me. I can't compete with a ghost.'

'What?' Her words resounded around his head. 'You think you're competing with Bonnie? Why on earth would you think that?'

'Because you won't let me in.' Her answer came back straight away. 'I need more. I want more. I want you to love me like I love you. We all have secrets, Iain. Things that we don't share with anyone but the people we love.'

His eyes fixed on the black flowing water, rushing and tumbling past them. This was it. It was time to tell Lexi the truth. They had no future together. But she had to know it was because of him—not because of her. And not because of a ghost.

'I don't deserve you, Lexi. I don't deserve anyone. All I do is hurt the people I love.'

Her brow wrinkled. 'This *is* about Bonnie, isn't it? Why on earth would you say that? You've told me about Bonnie, and about your children. That was a tragedy. A horrible thing to happen to anyone. But it was bad luck. Horrible, horrible bad luck. But why does that mean we can't have a chance?'

Her words were swimming through his head. Juggling back and forth with the blackness and feelings of guilt. The horrible weight of responsibility.

It was almost as if someone had pushed a little button, flicked a switch somewhere inside him. He couldn't think about the 'right' words to say.

He couldn't think at all. He had to get this over with. Once Lexi knew the truth she would happily walk away.

'*Because it was my fault!*' he yelled.

The words echoed through the inky black night, carrying along the dark path and beyond.

Lexi flinched backwards, shock stamped all across her face.

There was silence. Iain couldn't speak, he was surrounded by the steamy breath that he'd just shot out and his heart was pounding in his chest.

He said it. He'd got it out there. But instead of feeling the weight of relief he might have, he just wanted to crumple down into a ball. He'd lost his wife and children because of his selfish behaviour. Instead of protecting his family, he'd destroyed them completely. No wonder he had problems sleeping at night.

Lexi looked stunned. Her hand touched his sleeve. Her voice was quiet, almost whispering. 'How? How can it be your fault? Your wife died during childbirth.'

He squeezed his eyes shut. 'It's my fault because Bonnie had wanted to give up IVF. We'd already had two attempts and she was done. She'd had enough.' He opened his eyes again to face Lexi, pointing his finger at his chest. 'It's my fault because I persuaded her to give it one last go. We still had viable embryos. I wanted to give them a chance. I didn't stop and think about the effects on Bonnie—mentally and physically. I was so fixated on getting a family. I thought with my love and support we would be fine.'

It was like scraping an iron claw down her back, digging it deep into her delicate flesh. He had no idea how much those words hurt. She didn't believe it had been Iain's fault for a second. But he'd just revealed how fixated he was on a family. A family she could never provide. Yet another reason to leave.

'Are you honestly telling me that Bonnie was unhappy being pregnant?'

'What? Of course not. She was delighted. She was over the moon to fall pregnant. And when we found out she was having twins it made everything she'd ever gone through seem worthwhile.'

'So how does that make it your fault, Iain? Bonnie could have said no. She could have refused to be implanted again.'

'But she did, Lexi. I persuaded her. *I did.*' Even though he'd got the words out there, his frustration was still building in his chest. His voice was rising. 'If I had left Bonnie alone she would still be here. If I hadn't pushed for the final round of IVF Bonnie wouldn't have died. She'd still be alive. Still here to breathe. Still here to do the things she loved with the people she loved. Instead, I see her every night in my dreams. I see the panic on her face as she realises something is wrong, something is very wrong. I watch the monitors around her as she starts to bleed out and her blood pressure plummets. Amidst the panic in the room I hear her whisper to save the babies as she squeezes my hand. She believed in me, Lexi. She trusted me to save our children.'

He leaned against the barrier to the Thames, putting his head in his hands. His legs were shaking. He was back in that brightly lit room again. Filled with more doctors and midwives than he'd ever imagined. Every time he turned he was in someone's way. Watching the life drain out of his beloved wife, and watching the faces of the staff as they eventually delivered two still white babies.

'I don't deserve you, Lexi. I don't deserve *any-one*.' The words hissed out of his mouth.

He waited a moment then straightened up. Most of the anger had dissipated from his body, along with most of his energy. He stared at the black water. His shoulders sagged. He couldn't peel his eyes away from the dark, churning water. It matched his mood. 'You've no idea. To hear the words of the doctor telling you that he's so sorry about your wife and your children.' He turned to face her, to look into her blue eyes and catch the flutter of her sparkling dress in the cold breeze. His heart squeezed in his chest.

Lexi. His beautiful little butterfly. The first person he'd connected with in years. The first person he'd loved in years.

Words couldn't begin to describe the rage he'd felt when he'd seen Jack with his hands on Lexi. He hadn't been able to control himself. The red mist had just descended.

She was his. His. And he couldn't bear the thought of someone hurting her.

But what right did he have to defend her, a woman who could clearly defend herself?

And more importantly, what right did he have to expose her to his failings? He couldn't protect the woman he loved. Life had already proved that.

He couldn't do to her what he'd done to Bonnie. Lexi was the one bright thing in his life right now. He had to let her go. He couldn't drag her down with him.

Lexi was the equivalent of a shooting star. He wanted her to reach for the moon and be free to fly. She deserved someone who could love her wholeheartedly and give her the attention she deserved. In his eyes she was more beautiful than she could ever imagine. Just her smile was enough for him. The smile that reached straight up from her heart and made her eyes sparkle.

But her eyes weren't sparkling right now. Tears were marring her pretty face, tears of sadness and pity—pity he didn't deserve.

He inhaled deeply. She had to understand this wasn't about her at all. This was all about the encompassing guilt and grief that still filled him.

'You've no idea what it's like for the doctor to ask you if you had decided on names for your children.'

It was almost as if she could read his mind. She laid the palms of her hands on his chest. He felt his chest wall move against her. She knew. Lexi felt real empathy for people. It was the reason they reacted so well to her. Right now, she *knew*.

She knew how desperate he felt about naming his children without Bonnie. They'd had some provisional names but hadn't agreed on any. To name them without her—to spend the rest of his life wondering if Bonnie would have agreed with his choices—had felt like the final nail on the single oak and two white matching coffins.

'What did you call your children?'

She'd stayed exactly where she was. Touching him. Not running away in revulsion at his actions.

'Isla and Ross.' All he could see right now were the three red poppies etched on the grave.

Lexi nodded slowly. 'They are beautiful names. I'm sure that Bonnie would have loved them.' She looked up at him. 'I can't believe you've felt like this for the last few years. I can't believe you've not spoken to anyone about this. It was not your fault, Iain. It wasn't.' She stepped back and put some distance between them. 'I didn't know Bonnie but she wouldn't have blamed you for this. She wouldn't have wanted you to be crippled by guilt. Bonnie loved you, Iain—she loved you. She wouldn't have wanted this for you.' She held her arms out. 'She couldn't possibly.'

And there she was, holding her arms open towards him. And after all that she'd said tonight, it was like an unspoken invitation. One that he just couldn't take.

No matter how much he wanted to.

He stepped towards her. 'It's late. Let me walk you home.'

They stood under the streetlight and he could see the fleeting look in her eyes. The one that realised, no matter what he'd just revealed, there was no way forward for them. There was no noise. No sound. Just a drip of tears down her face.

He couldn't do it. He couldn't look at her. Otherwise he might cry too. Cry over the woman he'd already lost, and the woman he was about to lose.

'I can't offer you anything, Lexi. I've got nothing to give.'

He started to walk along the river path, giving her no option but to follow him or be left standing herself in the middle of the night. His gran would have killed him over his lack of manners. But right now he couldn't even think straight.

Her heels caught up with him and then slowed as she stopped herself from walking alongside him, deliberately leaving herself walking a few steps behind. Maybe it was better this way?

The streets of London had never seemed so long or so bleak. Every step seemed to go nowhere. All the streets looked the same. Her footsteps never wavered behind him. She didn't try to touch him or talk to him again.

What must she think of him? A thought flashed through his mind. If she quit right now, Leo would kill him.

Lexi was doing a spectacular job at the clinic. And work was the one thing that gave her confidence in her abilities. Maybe he should quit? Maybe he should just leave to let Lexi get on with her life and meet someone new.

The pain in his stomach was so sudden it almost stopped him dead. Lexi with someone else. Was that really what he wanted? And if that was really what he wanted, why did he want to be sick here and now?

All of a sudden her door loomed in front of him. He heard her fumble for her key and slot it into the lock. He couldn't even look at her.

She wasn't his. He couldn't hurt her any more. He had to get away. He caught one last whiff of her heady perfume, the one that had driven him nuts for weeks.

'I'm sorry,' he whispered as he walked away.

CHAPTER THIRTEEN

THE BIRDS WERE even earlier than usual, their singing causing thumps around her brain. She put her head under the pillow. But after a few minutes it hadn't helped.

Last night she'd cried herself to sleep after drinking two glasses of wine. She was bundled up in the fleeciest pyjamas she owned. March was still cold in London. She couldn't bear to wear one of the satin nightdresses she'd been wearing when she'd shared her bed with Iain. Even though they'd offered no warmth at all, she hadn't needed it. She'd had Iain to cuddle up to.

Her stomach turned over. Iain. The look in his eyes last night. At one point she'd thought if she'd touched him, her big, burly, handsome Scotsman might crumble.

Her heart ached for him. Now it was all out there. Now she knew everything. And it was all her fault.

Why had she pushed him? What had it achieved?

She'd pushed him for information she could have lived without knowing. He blamed himself. He'd spent the last few years blaming himself.

What must that feel like? What must it feel like to wake up every day feeling responsible for the deaths of your wife and children? No wonder he'd never managed to have another relationship. No wonder he'd told her he couldn't sleep at night.

Her stomach twisted again. There it was. His scent on her pillows. She was never going to be close enough to him to smell that again. She was never going to hold his hand. Feel his lips on hers. Feel his hands on her body.

She thumped her fist into the pillow. How could she work with him every day after all this? Some days he spent at Kate's. But at some point every day he would be in the clinic. In her work space. Just waiting for an unsuspecting moment when they would run into one another.

Maybe she should find another job? She clenched her eyes tightly shut. She loved her job.

More than loved it. It was one of the things she was most proud of. Her nomination for the award had just been the icing on the cake. Did she really want to leave the job she loved? Or could she really face having to see Iain on a daily basis? From what she knew of him, it would hurt him just as much as it hurt her.

She wrapped her hands around her stomach. Maybe this wasn't emotional pain, maybe this was real pain. It certainly felt that way.

The alarm sounded next to her head and she flung her pillow at it as she swung her legs out of bed. Normally she jumped out of the bed in the morning, anxious to get to work. This definitely wasn't going to be one of those days.

The sight that greeted her in the mirror wasn't a good one. Her skin was so pale it was almost translucent, the dark circles under her eyes made her look ten years older. Smudges all over her face revealed that the last thing she'd been thinking about last night had been removing her make-up. Her hair was a tangled mess. She picked up a lock and dropped it again. She didn't have a single hair product that could remedy this.

She switched on the shower. She wanted to wash everything away. All the questions she'd asked. All the things she'd been told. Every look of hurt and pain on Iain's face.

He hadn't even said goodbye last night. She'd just watched him walk back along the street with his head down.

She stepped into the shower. 'Owwww!' It was scalding. She stood in the corner of the cubicle and braved her hand underneath the flow to turn the dial. A few seconds later she stepped under the torrent of water, turning her face up to meet its blast.

Wash it all away. Wash it all away.

Seven gallons of conditioner and a tube of facial scrub later she stepped out. She pulled a sombre black suit from her cupboard, looked at it for a few minutes then flung it aside.

She reached in again, this time finding a form-fitting emerald-green dress. It was power dressing. And the last thing she felt like doing today.

She looked in the mirror again as she sat down

to dry her hair. Her make-up lay across the dressing-table. She lifted her chin and looked again, determination flooding through her.

If this was the end and if she was going out, she was going out fighting.

This will be a good day. She kept repeating the words in her head like a mantra as she walked along the street. It stopped her from bursting into tears. She was going to have to get used to this. There was no getting away from it, she was going to have to see Iain every day at work whether it broke her heart or not.

The first time was always the hardest. And she was absolutely determined no one would see her cry. She was a professional.

She did her best to sweep though the reception area of the clinic as quickly as possible. 'Hi, Lexi,' Mel, one of the receptionists on duty, called. 'I'm so sorry about last night.'

Her stiletto heels stopped abruptly. She spun round, trying to stop her mouth from gaping open. 'What?'

Mel stood up and walked over towards her, a

quizzical expression on her face. 'The awards, of course. We all thought you should have won.'

The panic subsided. She could breathe again. Just as well really, because a few other staff had emerged and were all looking at her.

She pasted a smile on her face. 'Oh, thanks for that. I was just happy to be there.'

Fiona, another receptionist, stood up from behind the desk and picked up a tabloid newspaper. 'You made the headlines.'

Lexi felt her blood run cold. She moved over to the desk and looked at the front page. 'Iain McKenzie's secret love—Lexi Robbins'. She let out a strangled gasp. 'What?'

Both receptionists laughed. 'It's a great picture, isn't it?' Mel gave her a sideways glance. 'You do look like a couple, by the way. And how on earth did you get our Scotsman into a kilt? He looks good enough to eat.'

'He phoned in this morning,' said Fiona. 'Something's came up. Asked me to cancel his appointments this morning. He's going to be stuck at the Lighthouse Hospital all day.'

Her mouth dried instantly. She couldn't speak

as her eyes scanned the article. 'Can I keep this?' she asked, trying not to crumple the paper beneath her grasp.

'Sure, I'll buy another one.'

'Thanks.' Her feet flew down the corridor until she reached her office and slammed the door behind her. No! This was the last thing she wanted.

In a way she felt a sense of relief. Iain wouldn't be here today. She wouldn't need to see him. She wouldn't need to face him. Maybe he hadn't even seen the paper—after all, she hadn't until she'd come to work this morning.

She sat behind her desk. The first thing that caught her attention was the picture.

It was in full colour, showing off Lexi's dress and Iain's kilt in all their glory. But the thing that had obviously captured the photographer's interest was the look that was passing between them. It was there for the whole world to see.

They were both smiling, looking straight into each other's eyes. Neither of them was looking at the camera. Iain's hand was wrapped around her waist and with his other he was holding her hand—right in front of her stomach.

And with a look like that between them…
She put her head on the desk and groaned. This would be a disaster. She started to read.

Internet sensation Dr Iain McKenzie attended the Dakota Jefferson Awards last night with Lexi Robbins, daughter of supermodel Penelope Crosby and chat show host Steve Robbins. Speculation was rising last night regarding their relationship.

It was apparent they only had eyes for each other as they spent most of the evening together and sneaked off early after the awards. Lexi was dressed in an as yet unidentified stylish designer dress, with Iain in a black and white kilt, revealing more of his now famous physique.

Lexi and Iain work together at the Hunter Clinic in Harley Street and she was nominated for one of the PR awards. But maybe this is her biggest PR coup of all?

Lexi launched the commercial featuring Iain McKenzie just a few days ago and it currently has over nineteen million views on the internet. Not much is known about Iain McKenzie, a thirty-five-year-old recon-structive plastic surgeon from Edinburgh. He was widowed following the death of his wife Bonnie three years ago.

Maybe Lexi Robbins has caught the biggest catch of all?

Could this really be any worse? Wait until Iain saw it, it made her sound as if she'd deliberately set out to catch him—all for the sake of publicity. Too bad her heart only functioned around Iain and not her brain. She couldn't have planned this if she'd tried.

The corners of her mouth turned up as she noticed a little picture down in the bottom corner of the piece. The one with her mother, her father and herself. Penelope would go ballistic. Of all the people in the world she'd expect to push her off the front page, Lexi would never be one. For the first time that day a tiny little surge of pleasure crept through her. It was childish, and she'd never say the words out loud, but just imagining the look on her mother's face this morning would be pleasure enough. It would make up for almost being completely ignored last night.

The moment passed. And the feeling of dread returned.

What would this mean for Iain? She was cringing just thinking about it. She knew exactly how invasive the media could be. It was a miracle that they'd never found out about her hysterectomy. What if they dug into Iain's background and found out about the death of his children? That would be awful.

There was a knock on the door, followed by some muffled sounds as someone struggled with the handle. Then a burst of rainbow colours entered the room.

It was the biggest display of flowers Lexi had ever seen. Absolutely beautiful. Red, pink, yellow and orange roses, carnations and tulips, white freesias, purple and white irises and masses of greenery. In between it all were silver strands, just like the sequins on her dress last night. It was like a veritable explosion of colour.

Carrie struggled to get them through the door and slid them across the desk towards Lexi, who was already on her feet. Her heart was thudding in her chest. She worked in PR and had seen massive bouquets before, but nothing like this.

'Wow, Lexi, aren't they gorgeous?' She handed over a card in a silver envelope. 'Hopefully this will make you feel a bit better.'

'What do you mean?' She stood with the card in her hand. Who would have sent her something like this? Her heart started thudding against her chest wall. It couldn't be—could it? Would Iain really make a gesture this big? No one at the clinic was supposed to know they were seeing each other. As far as everyone at work was concerned, Iain had gone along to the award ceremony because he'd nominated her. Nothing else. Until that picture in the newspaper this morning.

'I never got a chance to talk to you this morning, but you looked kinda sad. Are you upset about not winning last night?'

Lexi was startled by Carrie's question. Not winning was the last thing on her mind this morning. She hadn't even given it a second thought.

She shook her head firmly. 'No, not at all.'

'Then what is it?' Carrie walked around the desk and touched the tabloid at the corner of it. 'Is it this?'

She pointed to the photo of Iain and Lexi, holding hands and looking at each other as if no one else in the world existed.

It was automatic. The welling of tears in her eyes. She pulled the silver envelope apart and took out the card.

Next time it will be yours!
Love from Leo and your colleagues at the Hunter Clinic.
We're so proud you're part of our team. x

Iain. It wasn't from Iain. This wasn't some fairy story with a happy ending. A few tears escaped and slid down her cheeks.

Carrie walked behind her, reading the card over her shoulder. 'Oh, that's so nice, isn't it? Lexi? Don't be upset.'

She wrapped her arms around her friend and gave her a hug. There it was. The first tiny sign of life. The smallest little bump in her friend's abdomen.

She made a dive for the tissues on her desk to wipe her face and nose.

'I'm fine, Carrie. Really I am. It's just a lovely gesture.' She straightened up and touched the petal of one of the pink roses. 'And the flowers smell gorgeous.'

Carrie nodded. From the expression on her face it was clear that she knew something else was wrong but she was wise enough not to pry any further.

She pointed towards the office door. 'I've just made some coffee. I'll bring you some and then I'll shut the door, shall I? Give you some privacy to get on with your work.' The phones were ringing loudly outside. 'We've got about a hundred messages for you this morning, and just as many for Iain. Why don't I filter them and leave you both the ones that are appropriate?' She gave a little smile. 'I'm assuming that you two don't want to advertise baked beans on TV?'

Lexi let out a laugh. 'Really?'

Carrie nodded. 'Oh, yes. Some of the messages

will make your hair curl!' She counted off on her fingers. 'Dating companies, condom adverts, bra adverts, and a few very slimy offers of dates.'

Lexi let a shiver go down her spine. 'Oh, no, thanks. Yes, Carrie, filter away. I'd be very grateful.'

A few minutes later a strong coffee appeared on her desk followed by the sound of her door closing quietly. Carrie really was a good friend.

She scrolled through her emails, deleting many as she went along. Interview request after interview request. Some from very dubious sources. A few from journalists about her charity work. She swithered. Did they really want to know about the charity work or were they just looking at a way to get access to her private life and Iain? She knew exactly how some journalists worked.

She flagged a few and decided to talk to Leo about them. After all, this was his clinic and although she was Head of PR, they needed to agree their plans.

The next few emails made her eyes boggle. Men. Inviting her on dates. And that was just the polite ones. The others were enough to turn her lukewarm curls into tight spirals.

After that there was a whole host of congratulatory emails and a few invites to give lectures to university students on PR. One was from her own university and she replied instantly. Finally, she flagged the ones that were real work. There were a number of issues with the charities that would have to be dealt with promptly, so she put her head down and gave them her immediate attention.

A knock at the door startled her. She gave a sigh. It would probably be another member of staff coming to offer sympathy. It wasn't that she wasn't grateful, but they'd been popping in all morning and she still had a ton of work to get done.

She held her breath. Maybe if she didn't answer they would think she wasn't in. It wasn't exactly perfect behaviour, but it would get her work done more quickly.

The knock sounded again. Mr or Mrs Persistence was not going to be put off. The door opened and she tried to duck behind the flowers. She really didn't want to talk to anyone right now.

'Lexi?'

Her head shot back around the mountain of flowers. 'Iain?' Her reaction was automatic, she stood up. She wanted to cringe. He must have seen the papers. He was probably in here to complain.

It was all she could do not to drink in the sight of him. He wasn't supposed to be here all day, so she wasn't prepared. She hadn't gone over in her head what she would say to him about last night. How to apologise for pushing him for an answer he obviously wasn't ready to give.

Her eyes narrowed. 'Iain? Why have you got scrubs on?'

He stepped into the room and closed the door behind him. 'Because I didn't have time to get changed.'

She drew in a deep breath. Iain, in navy blue scrubs revealing tanned, muscled arms and the thin material brushing against his big thighs. His hair looked as if he had just released it from a theatre cap and run his fingers through it. There was a dark shadow along his chin and a few dark shadows around his eyes. He'd obviously slept as little as she had.

'Why didn't you have time to get changed?' she asked, trying not to wonder if this question was a smoking gun. Did he want her fired over all the publicity—all the assumptions the press had made?

He walked towards her. She couldn't read his face at all. All she could see was fatigue. But there was something else. Something she didn't expect at all.

There was sparkle in his eyes.

'I've been at the Lighthouse since six a.m. Emergency surgery on a child in a road accident. The NHS surgeons needed a hand as things were more complicated than they expected and their own plastic surgeon was at the burns unit with another child.'

She nodded. It might be slightly unusual but because of the reciprocal relationship between the clinic and the two hospitals, on rare occasions they were asked to help out.

'So what's the big rush that you couldn't get

changed?' She walked around the desk, her steps hesitant as she made her way towards him. 'Iain, is this about the newspapers? I'm so sorry about that. I've prepared a press release.' She lifted a piece of paper from her desk. 'I was just going to double-check with Leo before I put it out. Have you been harassed this morning?'

His brow wrinkled and he sat down in the chair opposite her with a sigh. 'Lexi, what are you talking about?'

She nodded at the tabloid on her desk.

He picked it up and started to read. Then something unexpected happened. Iain McKenzie flung back his head and laughed. The loudest laugh she'd ever heard from him.

'I bet your mother loved this,' he said, waving the paper at her.

Her heart jumped. He wasn't angry. He wasn't angry at all. Maybe he wasn't here to tear a strip off her after all.

She sat down in the chair next to him. 'Funnily enough, I haven't heard from her this morning.'

He raised his eyebrows. 'Now, there's a surprise.'

Her stomach was churning. Iain reached over and grabbed her lukewarm coffee, finishing it in one gulp.

She closed her eyes. He was too close. And she had no idea what was happening right now. 'I'm sorry, Iain.'

'You're sorry? Sorry about what?'

She took a deep breath and opened her eyes. 'I'm sorry about last night.' She indicated the paper. 'I'm sorry about that. I'm sorry about filming the advert and getting you so much unwanted attention.' She took another breath. 'And most of all I'm sorry about pushing you to tell me something you weren't ready to.'

Iain sat silent for a few minutes. 'I knew it, you're officially crazy.'

'What?' She couldn't believe it. What on earth was going on?

He stood up and pointed at the flowers. 'Tell me one thing. Should I be worried? Is someone else about to steal you away?'

She couldn't answer. She was flabbergasted. He walked around the monster bouquet and knelt in front of her.

He stared up at her with his big brown eyes. 'Because I want you to know, Lexi Robbins, I'll fight to the death for you,' he whispered.

This time her breath caught in her throat. 'They're from Leo,' she said hoarsely, 'and the rest of the staff at the clinic.'

'You don't know how glad I am to hear that. Lexi, honey, you have nothing to be sorry for. Not a single thing.' He reached out and took her hand.

'Wh-what do you mean?' Her voice was trembling. Her hands were trembling too.

Iain looked different this morning. And that didn't include the scrubs. He looked as if the weight of the world had been lifted off his shoulders. There wasn't a brooding black cloud hanging over him. There was sadness in his eyes, but it was different. It was focused entirely on *her*. Not on someone else.

His hand closed firmly around hers. 'I mean that I'm the one who should be sorry. And I'm the one who should be thanking you.'

She shook her head. 'I don't get it. What's happened?'

'I don't get it either. But I know who got me here.' He stood up, pulling her into his arms.

'From the first second I met you, no, from the first second I smelled you, you started to wake me up. You started to make me *feel* again.'

She didn't know what to say. This was so un-expected. And she was scared. He was touching her, holding her. But after last night she couldn't believe it was true.

'Iain, what's going on here?'

He lifted his hand and ran a gentle finger down her cheek. 'It's you, Lexi Robbins. This is all about you.'

Her hand reached up and covered his. She was still trembling, she couldn't help it. Had she fallen asleep at her desk? Was she in the middle of a dream? This really couldn't be happening.

Iain's warm breath was on her skin. She could smell his scent with every breath she took. 'Lexi, you're the bravest woman I've ever met. Even with the parents you have—and the bad experi-ence of Jack Parker—you have never given up on love. Last night, when you weren't afraid to tell me you wanted more. You *deserve* more. I realised exactly what I could lose if I couldn't stop being afraid.'

She shook her head. 'You're not afraid of things, Iain. You're just not ready.'

He smiled. 'I thought I wasn't ready. But my body...' he pointed at his chest '...and heart were telling me something different.' He ran his fingers down her arms and put his hands back at her waist. 'Last night helped me gain some perspective. I finally said the words out loud. I've waited a long time for that.'

She couldn't help it. No matter how confused she was feeling right now, she couldn't stay away. She wound her arms around his neck and held him close. Their breathing unified. Up and down at the same time. They stayed like that for a few minutes.

If only time could just stop here. If only she could stay in this moment for ever. This could be perfect.

But it wasn't. It couldn't be.

Iain was having an epiphany in his life. He had hopes and dreams. And she was about to dash some of them because she'd been so focused on him telling her the truth that she hadn't done it herself.

She pulled back a little and touched his cheek just below his dark eyes. This was where she wanted to stay. This was who she wanted to stay with. He was smiling at her now. Capturing her heart the way he'd captured the heart of all the women watching the advertisement. Iain could do that to you, with just one look.

'I'm so glad you finally said those words,' she whispered. 'You would have been a wonderful father.' Would he hear the sadness in her tone? Would he understand when she told him she didn't want to steal that opportunity from him?

But Iain looked happy, his skin was brighter and his eyes positively shining. His voice lowered, taking on a quiet tone. 'Bonnie loved me, Lexi. I can say that with pride. And I loved her. We *both* wanted that family together.'

This was it. This was where everything she wanted fell apart.

'She wouldn't have wanted this for me. She would have wanted me to move on.' His eyes lowered to meet hers. 'She would have wanted me to be happy. Happy with you.'

She took a step back, out of his embrace. Her head was starting to swim. She'd never been the type to go weak at the knees, but right now she felt as if she was about to take a swan dive. She thumped down into the chair behind her.

'Don't, Iain. Don't do this.' She closed her eyes tightly.

'What's wrong? What do you mean?' He knelt down in front of her again. His face still had that exuberant look about it. He was still caught up in the moment. Thinking that they could both have their happy-ever-after. 'Do you know what I dreamed about last night, Lexi?'

He didn't give her a chance to answer.

'You. I dreamed about you. It's not the first time and it won't be the last. But now I can go to sleep knowing that I won't be haunted by nightmares. Now I know that when I close my eyes it's going to be good memories and a happy future.'

She bit her lip. She had to stop him. She had to stop him now. Before he said that those dreams were filled with their children dancing beside them.

She lifted her hand. 'Stop, Iain. Just stop.'

He pulled back a little. 'What's wrong?'

Tears started to flow down her cheeks. 'I don't want you to tell me the next part. I'm not the woman for you. We're not going to sail off into the sunset with a family around us.'

'Lexi? Lexi, what's wrong?' He leaned forward and put his hands on her shoulders. 'Why are you crying? What is it?'

She lifted one of his hands off her shoulder and pressed it to her stomach, her hand over his. 'I can't give you your dream, Iain. I can't give you the family that you want.'

She started to sob. Now she'd started crying she didn't know how to stop.

'Lexi?' His voice had deepened but he didn't sound angry, he sounded concerned.

She fumbled for her bag and pulled out a dog-eared photograph and pushed it towards him. He picked it up and squinted at it, before placing it on her lap.

'It's you. With a baby. You look so young.

What are you telling me?' The concern was laced all through his voice.

She sniffed. 'I told you that my Aunt Josephine looked after me for a while?'

He nodded.

'She is the wisest woman I've ever known. When I had my accident I was only twelve. Horses can do a lot of damage to a young body.'

He nodded seriously but said nothing, letting her continue.

She tried to brush away some of her tears. 'I had a hysterectomy, Iain. I had a hysterectomy when I was twelve. I'm never going to be able to give you the children that you want.'

She pointed to the photo. 'This is my life. This is how I will get my family. My aunt knew straight away what she was doing when she took me to that orphanage. She was showing me that there were children who needed love. Children who needed families. Children all over the world who could benefit from being adopted.' She met his eyes. 'That's the only way I can get the family I want.'

His face broke into a smile. 'And why is that so awful? Why is that something to cry about?'

'Because it's not your only option.' The words shot out of her mouth. She didn't mean them to sound bitter. But it was the thing that was front and foremost in her mind.

He touched her face again, brushing away her tears. 'The option that I want is you.'

Her voice still trembled. 'But you deserve so much more.' Her eyes were heavy with tears and although she was scared to look at him she had to.

He stood over her, looking at her with his deep chocolate eyes with sincerity radiating from them. 'What I hope I deserve—if you're willing to forgive me—is you. You—Lexi Robbins—are the most important person to me in the world right now.'

His voice was so sincere, so solid that she took in a shuddery breath. She'd thought he would want a family too much to stay with her. 'But—'

He put his finger across her lips. 'But nothing. I watched you at the Tower. You will make some lucky children a fabulous mother. And I really hope above everything that I can make a good dad. You've got years' worth of contacts with your orphanage in China. I have contacts with the orphanage I'm going back to in Romania this summer. If there is a way to make this happen, Lexi, we will.' He wound her hair around his fingers, cradling her head in his hands. 'And if for some reason it doesn't, then I'll still be the happiest man alive, growing old with the woman I love.'

Lexi's eyes widened. Her whole body was starting to shake. 'Iain?'

He knelt down on one knee in front of her, pulling a pale blue box from his scrubs pocket. 'I've been an idiot. I've had the most wonderful, bravest woman that I know right in front of me for the last six weeks. And it's about time I shouted to the world how proud I am of her. Lexi Robbins, will you do me the honour of being my wife?' He shifted on his knees as he held the box out towards her. 'In sickness and in health, for better or worse, for richer or poorer?'

He flipped open the box. A beautiful high-set single heart-shaped diamond.

She was shaking as he gave her a smile, a wink and continued. He nodded to the dog-eared photo sitting on the desk. 'I promise to love you even if you don't use frizz-prevention products on your hair.'

She drew in a mock sharp breath as her face broke into a smile at his cheeky comment.

'I promise to love you when you tell kids scary stories at the Tower of London.' He pulled the ring from the box and started to slide it onto her finger. 'I promise to love you when you get soaked in the rain and your running mascara makes your face like a panda's. And I promise to love you and tell you how gorgeous you are every time you get a little sad.'

Her heart was going to burst. Iain did things in his style—and that's what she loved most about him.

She stared at the beautiful ring on her finger. She couldn't have picked anything more perfect herself.

He winked at her again. 'You could take your mother's eye out with that.'

'I certainly could.' She stood up, reaching for

his hand and pulling him up with her. She gave him her gravest look. 'I have some conditions, Iain.'

He straightened his shoulders, but the amused look on his face didn't change. He was happy. He was truly happy right now, and it just radiated from him. His warmth was spreading to her. Skimming across her skin and wrapping her up in his happy glow. A lifetime of feeling like this? She'd be a fool not to say yes.

She'd be a fool not to say yes to the man she loved with her whole heart.

Although she'd known for a long time she couldn't have children naturally, here was a man who was—come what may—willing to take that journey with her. She would love to be a mother, just as much as he would love to be a father. But no matter where that journey led, they would take it together.

She reached up to touch his shaggy hair. 'You have to promise me never to cut your hair. I love it.'

He nodded solemnly. 'I do.'

She nearly let out a laugh at his response. 'Are you practising?' she whispered. He nodded.

'You have to promise me that when we get married it will be a tiny wedding. No publicity. No newspapers and…' she rolled her eyes '…definitely not my parents. Your parents, absolutely.'

His eyebrows lifted. 'I do.'

She bent down and ran her hand up the length of his thin navy scrubs. She could see him arch his back, his body responding instantly to her touch. 'You have to promise me you'll wear a kilt.'

'Aha…' He hesitated.

She quirked her head at him. She'd been expecting the 'I do' response.

'In that case…' His hands came down to her hips, pulling her up close against him. Letting her see exactly what she did to him. 'You have to promise to wear your gorgeous dress from last night. I've never seen anyone look so lovely, and that's just what I want my bride to wear. Like a beautiful butterfly.'

She wrapped her arms around his neck. 'I

think I can do that.' Her blue eyes were fixed on his. She didn't want to wait. She didn't want to wait a second to marry her gruff Scotsman. 'Marylebone Registry Office?'

Iain smiled. The small registry office was obviously exactly what he had in mind. 'Random strangers from the street?'

'Sounds perfect to me.' And then he picked her up and twirled her round. Her left hand was on his shoulder and the sunlight caught her enormous ring, causing a beautiful rainbow of sparkles to reflect all around them.

He smiled when he saw them. 'Guess who just got to the end of the rainbow,' he whispered, as he set her down and kissed her like he'd never kissed her before.

* * * * *

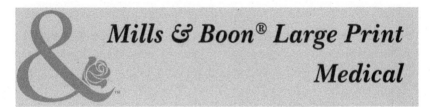

Mills & Boon® Large Print
Medical

November

200 HARLEY STREET: THE PROUD ITALIAN	Alison Roberts
200 HARLEY STREET: AMERICAN SURGEON IN LONDON	Lynne Marshall
A MOTHER'S SECRET	Scarlet Wilson
RETURN OF DR MAGUIRE	Judy Campbell
SAVING HIS LITTLE MIRACLE	Jennifer Taylor
HEATHERDALE'S SHY NURSE	Abigail Gordon

December

200 HARLEY STREET: THE SOLDIER PRINCE	Kate Hardy
200 HARLEY STREET: THE ENIGMATIC SURGEON	Annie Claydon
A FATHER FOR HER BABY	Sue MacKay
THE MIDWIFE'S SON	Sue MacKay
BACK IN HER HUSBAND'S ARMS	Susanne Hampton
WEDDING AT SUNDAY CREEK	Leah Martyn

January

200 HARLEY STREET: THE SHAMELESS MAVERICK	Louisa George
200 HARLEY STREET: THE TORTURED HERO	Amy Andrews
A HOME FOR THE HOT-SHOT DOC	Dianne Drake
A DOCTOR'S CONFESSION	Dianne Drake
THE ACCIDENTAL DADDY	Meredith Webber
PREGNANT WITH THE SOLDIER'S SON	Amy Ruttan

Mills & Boon® Large Print
Medical

February

TEMPTED BY HER BOSS	Scarlet Wilson
HIS GIRL FROM NOWHERE	Tina Beckett
FALLING FOR DR DIMITRIOU	Anne Fraser
RETURN OF DR IRRESISTIBLE	Amalie Berlin
DARING TO DATE HER BOSS	Joanna Neil
A DOCTOR TO HEAL HER HEART	Annie Claydon

March

A SECRET SHARED...	Marion Lennox
FLIRTING WITH THE DOC OF HER DREAMS	Janice Lynn
THE DOCTOR WHO MADE HER LOVE AGAIN	Susan Carlisle
THE MAVERICK WHO RULED HER HEART	Susan Carlisle
AFTER ONE FORBIDDEN NIGHT...	Amber McKenzie
DR PERFECT ON HER DOORSTEP	Lucy Clark

April

IT STARTED WITH NO STRINGS...	Kate Hardy
ONE MORE NIGHT WITH HER DESERT PRINCE...	Jennifer Taylor
FLIRTING WITH DR OFF-LIMITS	Robin Gianna
FROM FLING TO FOREVER	Avril Tremayne
DARE SHE DATE AGAIN?	Amy Ruttan
THE SURGEON'S CHRISTMAS WISH	Annie O'Neil